TEATIME PASTRIES AND PUNISHMENTS

TEATIME CLASSIC WHODUNIT COZY MYSTERY
BOOK 1

LEIGHANN DOBBS

SUMMARY

A classic English village whodunit that combines characters from two of *USA Today* bestselling-author Leighann Dobbs's most beloved series in a humorous mystery that will keep you guessing until the end.

A dead body in the koi pond of the Twigsledge Flower Show is nothing unusual for amateur sleuth Ida Johnston, who is vacationing in the English village where the show is being held. She's sure she can solve the crime before afternoon tea, especially since she already has her first suspect—the strange cat-attracting woman who is staying in the cottage next door.

Elspeth Whipple is no slouch when it comes to solving

murders either. It hasn't escaped her notice that the odd, scone-stealing woman in the cottage next to hers doesn't seem to be disturbed by the body. Could that be because the woman put it there?

When their amateur sleuthing lands them on the radar of the local police, the two women are forced to team up in order to clear their names. Finding the killer is no easy task, however, especially when the entire village had reason to want the victim dead.

This stand-alone mystery combines characters from the Mystic Notch Cozy Mystery series and the Lexy Baker Cozy Mystery series and is perfect for fans of *Miss Marple*, *Midsomer Murders*, and *Murder, She Wrote*.

CHAPTER 1

A sweet floral scent hung in the early-morning air as Elspeth Whipple surveyed the colorful flowers covering the small backyard of the quaint English village cottage where she was vacationing. Sunshine warmed the patio stones and enhanced the vibrant rainbow hues of the petunias, delphiniums, hollyhocks, primroses, and phlox that overflowed the edges of the garden and spilled from the dozens of planters around the patio. Fat bumblebees buzzed from flower to flower. Birds chirped as they hopped around the flower beds and flew between planters.

The orange-striped tomcat that had been hanging around since she'd arrived jumped up on the stone wall that divided her patio from the cottage next door and eyed her curiously. The orange cat wasn't the only one that had been frequenting the backyard, as there was a gray cat and a brown-and-black-striped cat as well. The cats reminded Elspeth of Mystic Notch, the town in the White Mountains of New Hampshire that she called home.

Back home, Elspeth was known for taking in stray cats. She had a whole gang of them in her barn. She often felt as if she could actually communicate with them, and she couldn't pass up a chance to get to know a strange cat. She crouched down and made little noises, trying to get the orange cat to come to her, but just as he started to come close, a sound on the path that meandered behind the cottage scared him away.

Elspeth straightened, trying to see who was approaching, but a six-foot-tall trellis crammed with lush pink roses blocked the view.

She couldn't see who was walking down the path, but she could hear them, and whoever they were sounded most agitated.

"...village as we know it will be changed." A man's harsh whisper floated over the wall. "And not for the better."

"Don't worry." This voice was a woman's. "I have fixed things so the project will never happen."

"How could you possibly do that?" The man sounded incredulous but intrigued.

"Leave that to me. Our quaint village life will be ruined over my dead body!"

The fierce tone of the woman's voice set off warning bells for Elspeth, and she hurried over to peek through the flowers to see who it was. Unfortunately, the leaves were too dense and the branches covered with thorns. By the time she'd moved enough aside to peek through, the couple was long gone.

"Now what was that about?" Elspeth asked out loud. She had a sneaking suspicion it had something to do with the sale of the big mansion, Crowley Hall, that dominated the town. She'd heard rumors of a golf course and hotel being put in, and from what she'd heard in the tea shop, the villagers were not very happy about that.

She couldn't blame them. The old hall had been there for hundreds of years. Sitting across from the town green, it was the central point in the village and the location of the Twigsledge Flower Show, a huge yearly event that drew people from all over the world. The flower show was one of the reasons Elspeth had come to the village, and she planned to be one of the first at the gate when it opened this morning.

Speaking of which, Elspeth needed to get ready.

The show would start in an hour, and she didn't want to miss a bit of it. As she turned to walk back to her cottage, a movement next door at Thistle Cottage caught her eye.

The white-haired woman who inhabited that cottage was poking her head out the window, looking right at Elspeth. Elspeth had seen the woman in the village before. Like Elspeth, she was visiting from the States and also appeared to be in her early eighties.

Their eyes locked. The woman's gaze narrowed, and her lips pursed just before she abruptly pulled her head back inside and shut the window.

No doubt about it, the woman was odd. Just yesterday in the tea shop, Elspeth had seen her sneaking a scone into her purse.

Weird behavior, indeed. There was something not right about that peculiar woman in Thistle Cottage, and Elspeth couldn't help but wonder if the disturbing conversation she'd heard on the path had anything to do with her.

IDA JOHNSTON STOOD BACK from the window and reflected on the strange snippet of conversation she'd just heard. Not that she'd been eavesdropping—one could hardly help but overhear if people whispered loudly enough for the voices to drift through an open window.

She wasn't quite sure what the conversation was about. Some sort of change to the quaint village where she was vacationing, but if you asked her, the tone of the voices indicated something nefarious was afoot. Ida considered herself to be somewhat of an expert on nefarious activities. She was a key member of the Ladies' Detective Club back in Brook Ridge Falls, New Hampshire, where she lived in a retirement community. She and her three friends—Mona, Ruth, and Helen—were quite well known for solving mysteries, and Ida was the brains of the whole operation. Of course, she let the others, especially Mona, think they were the brains, but Ida knew it was usually she who figured out the best clues.

She glanced out through the cross-hatched panes of the cottage window to see a black cat skulking across the patio of the cottage next door.

The woman in the cottage next door was an odd one. She was always out there talking to the cats. One time Ida had seen her in the middle of the night, gazing up at the full moon. And where did all those cats come from? It was almost as if the woman attracted them. At least they kept to her cottage. The last thing Ida wanted was a bunch of cats coming around, begging for pieces of scones or bites of the delicious seed cakes that they served at the tea shops.

It was no surprise, given the woman's strange behavior, that Ida had seen her at the back of the property where the voices had come from. Ida knew the owners of the mysterious voices had been walking the path that ran along the back of the property. Too bad she couldn't see them, though, because the path was hidden from her view by the tall brick wall at the end of her patio.

But the woman in the next cottage had been down near the path, and her cottage didn't have a wall, just a tall trellis. Had she been one of the people speaking? If not, why was she so close to the path? Her rose-laden trellis created a boundary, but what if she was one of the whisperers? Ida wouldn't put it past her to be up to something sneaky.

The thought would have given a normal person pause but not Ida. In fact, Ida wouldn't mind if something unusual *did* happen. When she'd booked the vacation, she'd thought that spending her days drinking tea and attending the big flower show in the village would be relaxing, but it turned out that English village life could be a bit boring.

At least today the flower show would open and

she'd have something to occupy her brain, she thought as she sat down at the old pine table and pulled a napkin-wrapped scone out of her large, patent-leather purse.

The scone had come from the tea shop in town, a quaint little place that served proper English tea and three-tiered plates of cakes and small crustless sandwiches. It wasn't stealing—she'd already paid for it and didn't want it to go to waste. Besides, that was what she usually did with the pastries from the Cup and Cake, the bakery owned by Mona's granddaughter back home.

She sat back and munched on the scone. It was still quite tasty despite having been in her purse overnight. Glancing at the iPad on the table, she thought about her friends. She'd FaceTimed them the day before, and they'd claimed they didn't have a new case. But Ida couldn't be sure they weren't just lying to her because they felt sorry for her.

Just as well. They could hardly solve a case without me. Might as well enjoy myself while I'm here, she thought as she glanced around the cottage. It really was quaint, just like you would see on British television, with low ceilings and beams, a big fireplace, wooden floors, and antique furniture that looked like it had been in the cottage for two hundred years.

She was looking forward to the flower show. She'd been a bit of a gardening enthusiast before she'd moved into her apartment at the Brook Ridge Retirement Center, and even though she didn't have a yard, she had a balcony and could put out planters. She might get some tips on how to be successful with those here at the show.

She pushed up from the table and brushed the crumbs off her fingers. Plenty of time to look for a new case when she got back to New Hampshire.

CHAPTER 2

*E*lspeth patted her white bun into place and shut the gate to the front walkway of her cottage. The flower show was at the enormous estate in the heart of the village and within walking distance. There was barely any car traffic in the village. Lots of bicycles, though. She'd have to remember to be on the lookout for those. She walked to the end of the street where there was a roundabout with a grassy area in the middle.

She looked to her left just to make sure nothing was coming then stepped into the road as she looked to the right.

Honk!

A small car raced past, and she stepped back. *Darn it!* She'd forgotten they drove on the other side over here. Apparently there were no speed limits either, judging by how fast that car was going. Walking around the roundabout wasn't very appealing, so perhaps she should cut through the grassy area. There were unusually tall daisies growing in the middle, and she wanted a better look at them anyway. This time she looked both ways and then crossed the street.

The grass was shiny with dew, and she hesitated. She had brand-new canvas sneakers on and didn't want them to get all wet lest they stain. Then again, she really did want a look at those daisies. She had a perfect spot for something that tall in her garden, and daisies would go nicely with the other flowers already planted. She wanted a closer look and to take a picture of them with her smartphone.

Oh well, the shoes would probably dry pretty quickly. She plunged into the grass, disrupting the shiny dewed blades with dark footprints. When she got to the center, she noticed a lovely display of purple cone flowers and black-eyed Susans mixed in with the white and yellow daisies. Someone else had been there about an hour before. She could see the faint impression of footprints and wheelbarrow tracks from the opposite side of the roundabout where the flower show was set up. Apparently someone had picked some, though she couldn't say she blamed them. There were plenty here and would make a lovely arrangement in a vase.

She took her pictures and headed across, walking in the tracks already made, to the entry gate of the show where a bit of a crowd had already gathered.

Elspeth paid the fee and waited to have her hand stamped for re-entry. The flower show was at the grounds at Crowley Hall, which Elspeth understood were normally lovely with extensive gardens. For the show, more plants, displays, and plantings had been brought in. Flowers bloomed everywhere. Trellises, arbors, and whimsical potting sheds were dotted about the expansive estate. There must have been an acre or more on display, and every object you could imagine was covered in colorful blooms whose scents spiced the air.

In the center, tents had been set up for judging the various flower contests. Elspeth had heard that Sir John, the owner of Crowley Hall, was an orchid enthusiast and favored to win first place in the orchid contest himself.

The tents also held various baked goods for sale, but Elspeth passed by the delicious-looking homemade cakes, cookies, and cupcakes with hardly a glance. She wanted to take in the show first and then seek out the tea tent and relax with a cup of something herbal and perhaps one of those lovely little cucumber sandwiches they offered in all the tea shops.

Taking out the map she'd been handed when she entered, she proceeded to the back, thinking to start there and then make her way toward the tents in the front by mid-morning. She passed under an archway covered with a lush orange trumpet vine, admiring the bright orange of the flowers.

At the back edge of the show was a giant koi pond edged with large stones. Elspeth couldn't tell whether it had been built for the show or was part of the gardens at the hall. The sound of water trickling in from a small waterfall had drawn people closer, and a crowd stood around, peering in, trying to spot a koi. Spotting one, however, was nearly impossible, because the surface of the pond was a mass of large pond lilies, their purple flowers in full bloom. The display was beautifully tranquil, but no fish could be seen.

As she stepped to the edge, Elspeth briefly thought about how her cats at home would love to dip their paws into a koi pond. A pig-tailed girl wearing a pink polka-dotted skirt pushed in front of her, rushing to the edge of the pond. She leaned over the rocks and stuck her hand in.

"Lucy, don't touch!" The harried mother hurried to the child's side. She was too late, though; Lucy had cleared away the pads and was balancing precariously on the stones, her face practically touching the water.

"Look, Mommy, the fish!"

The mother grabbed the back of the child's shirt, and just in the nick of time, too, as it looked like she was about to topple in.

"Now, what have I told you about touching things?" The mother set the child in front of her, both hands on her shoulders. Poor Lucy stood there pouting, eyes cast down at the ground. Elspeth felt sorry for her.

"I'm sorry, Mommy. I just wanted to see the fish."

"You could hurt something." The mother's voice was gentler. "Look, you spilled the water. The fish need that water." The woman pointed to a large damp spot in front of where the child had moved the pads.

Elspeth frowned. Water had been spilled but not from the child. No, it looked like a large amount of water had been spilled sometime earlier. A few hours at least, Elspeth estimated judging by the drying mud. That was odd because the show had just opened only an hour ago. Perhaps they'd spilled the water while setting up? But the pond must have been here longer than this morning. Surely it was a fixture on the estate. One couldn't just set up a koi pond in one morning.

Elspeth moved closer. Yes, there certainly had been

a lot of water spilled. It was almost as if something had fallen or been thrown in. She peered into the pond. The lily pads were starting to move back together, but she saw a flash of orange and white as a large koi swam past. The thing must have been a foot long!

But then she saw something else, something that should not have been there. She pushed the pads out of the way and gasped when a face stared up at her from the water.

"There's a body in there!" the woman beside her shrieked.

"What? Surely you're mistaken." The woman's husband peered in over Elspeth's shoulder, then he also gasped. "Someone call the police!"

The crowd broke into a panic, some pushing forward to look into the pond, others running away.

Two younger gentlemen reached in and pulled the body out, laying it on the ground and trying to give it CPR.

"Someone call an ambulance!" a voice yelled, even as the sound of sirens split the air.

"I'm afraid it's too late for that."

Elspeth turned toward the voice. Something about the calm inquisitiveness of it set her on edge, so it should have been no surprise that the voice belonged to the strange woman from Thistle Cottage.

The woman, who was looking at the body with an inappropriate twinkle of excitement in her sharp blue eyes, continued. "This man is already clearly dead, and not only that… he's been murdered."

IDA ASSESSED the body with the keen eye of a seasoned investigator. One would think a lady of her age would be horrified, but she'd seen a few bodies in her day. This one had been hit on the side of the head. Must have fallen into the koi pond, which explained the damp ground. She couldn't be precisely sure by the condition of the body, but it seemed to her that it hadn't been in the pond long, maybe an hour or two. Certainly not days, as it would have floated to the top by then. Lucky thing for the killer that the lily pads covered the surface, otherwise the body would have been discovered earlier. But as it was, the killer had ample time to make their getaway.

Ida glanced at the woman from Hyacinth Cottage, who was also assessing the body. Odd for an old lady like herself to be so interested in a dead person. But then the lady *was* odd, all that business with the cats. When had her neighbor left for the flower show? Ida was sure she'd already been gone when Ida left about a half hour ago, but had she been here long enough to commit a murder? It wouldn't be the first time that a killer returned to the scene of the crime, though how would she have killed the man without being seen? The murder must have occurred prior to the opening of the show, but it would have been easy to get to the koi pond from the thickly wooded area just beyond, and there were no gates or fences to keep anyone out, just some velvet ropes. She supposed the show operated on the honor system, that most would go through the gates and pay the fee.

Ida narrowed her gaze at the strange woman. She fit all the criteria of a suspect. New to town. Odd behavior with cats. And last but not least, she'd found the body. Was that because she'd known exactly where to look? All Ida needed now was a motive. Perhaps a past association...

"It's Sir John!" A woman gasped, her hand flying to her mouth.

Didn't Sir John own the gigantic mansion that hosted the flower show? Hadn't there been some talk of him selling? Yes... someone was planning to turn it into a hotel and golf course, if Ida's memory served. And she was willing to bet that might make some people murderously unhappy.

"Step aside. Give us room!"

The police pushed into the gathering crowd. Ida was curious to see what the process was over here in England. Apparently much the same as in the States, judging by the way the uniformed men were encouraging the onlookers to move along, and the plainclothes detectives were focusing on the crime scene.

One of the detectives was a middle-aged woman wearing a tan trench coat. She looked a bit frumpy, like a housewife who suddenly decided she wanted to go back to work. Apparently she was the one in charge, though Ida couldn't understand why, as it appeared she was a bit slow on the uptake, just standing over the body and mulling things over. Her cohort was a younger man in his thirties, tall and lean, not too bad on the eyes and brimming with energy.

The man reminded her of Jack, the police detective back home whom they sometimes worked with. Ida and the Ladies' Detective Club had won his confidence with their investigatory skills, and he often asked them to consult on cases. Of course, it didn't hurt that he was married to Mona's granddaughter, Lexy, but that was beside the point.

Unfortunately, for this case, Ida wouldn't have time to establish the confidence of the local police. She'd have to get the information on the case the old-fashioned way—by eavesdropping.

The uniformed officer was making his way toward her, so she pretended to fiddle with something in her purse, dropping an old folded plastic rain bonnet on the ground in a stalling tactic. As she made a show of slowly bending toward the ground, she strained to hear the plainclothes detectives.

"I suppose we should notify the wife," the man was saying.

"Yes... the wife." The frumpy woman's voice sounded as if she were actually thinking of something else. Breakfast, perhaps. "Makes me wonder what might be in the will."

The man snorted. "Anyone's guess. Sir John was a widower and remarried to a much younger woman."

The trench-coat-clad woman's brows shot up. "That's right. He has a daughter, right? As I recall, she didn't approve of the marriage."

Ida's brain whirled with possibilities. A young wife? A daughter that didn't approve? A will? Yes, she would need to find out more about all of these things. And what better place than at the tea tent? That was where all the village gossip would be.

She snatched up the rain bonnet, noticing there was something else on the ground beside it. A small lipstick, similar to the decades-old Avon samples in her vanity drawer. A wrinkled hand reached out to pick up the lipstick, and Ida turned her head, coming eye to eye with the suspicious woman from Hyacinth Cottage! She was using the same stalling maneuver!

The other woman stared at her with suspicious eyes for a few beats before straightening and heading off.

Ida shoved the rain bonnet into her purse just as the policeman came around to her. He took her elbow. "Do you need help, ma'am?"

Ida smiled her helpless old-lady smile at him.

"Dear me. Such a terrible thing." She glanced back over her shoulder as the policeman led her away from the body. The two detectives were bent over the body, their voices lowered. There would be no more eavesdropping today. She'd have to get her information from the village gossips. "Could you point me toward the tea tent? I'm afraid all this excitement has rattled my nerves."

The policeman pointed down a path, and Ida hurried off, barely noticing the abundance of flowers spilling from planters that lined the way. She hadn't a moment to waste; a killer was on the loose.

CHAPTER 3

The tea tent was abuzz when Elspeth arrived. Nothing like a murder to get tongues wagging. She found a seat at a small, unoccupied table for two and ordered a soothing herbal tea and some shortbread. Then she perched on the edge of the metal folding chair and listened to the conversations around her while she pretended to be busy with her tea.

She already had a few suspects on her list, not the least of which was the woman from Thistle Cottage. Elspeth couldn't imagine what the woman's motive would be, but she certainly was acting suspicious. She'd dropped that silly, old-fashioned rain bonnet on purpose, so she could linger and listen in on the police. Of course, Elspeth had done the same with a tube of lipstick, but that didn't mean she could cross the other woman off her list.

She caught snatches of conversations from the crowd. A young wife. A disgruntled daughter. No mention of any enemies, but that might come with some prodding. Back home, Elspeth hardly got the chance to investigate anymore. In her younger days, she and her friend Anna had been quite good at it, but now that her friend was gone, she left most of that up to Anna's granddaughters, Willa and Gus. Of course, she still managed to control some things from behind the scenes, but that wasn't nearly as much fun, and she looked forward to exercising her investigatory skills here with this village murder.

"Excuse me, is this seat taken?" An ample-bosomed woman about Elspeth's age pointed at the other chair pulled up to Elspeth's table. She had a village accent. A local? Perhaps Elspeth could get some information from her.

"Please sit. I could use the company." Elspeth gestured to the chair.

The woman set her cup of tea on the table, pulled the chair out, and sat down.

"Shortbread?" Elspeth pushed the plate loaded with the tasty treat toward the woman who picked one out.

"Are you visiting from the States?" the woman

asked, clearly pegging Elspeth as a foreigner by her accent.

"Yes." Elspeth stuck her hand out. "Elspeth Whipple. From New Hampshire."

"Violet Crosby." The woman had a pleasant handshake. She took a sip of tea, peering at Elspeth over the rim of her cup with a flicker of guarded suspicion. "So, what brings you to our lovely village? Relatives? Friends?"

Elspeth got the impression she wasn't just being neighborly. The woman had a motive for coming over. Perhaps she was doing her own investigating. Elspeth smiled at the thought of being one of her suspects. "I came for the flower show, actually. I'm staying in Hyacinth Cottage."

"That's a lovely cottage! And the flower show is quite an event." Violet glanced around the full tent. "People come to our humble village from all over the world."

"I know." Elspeth frowned. "Everything is decorated up so lovely. I do hope the murder doesn't cast the show in a bad light."

"No matter, it's the last year anyway," Violet said sadly.

"It is?"

Violet's lips pursed as if the topic left a bad taste in her mouth. "Once the sale of Crowley Hall goes through, the new owners will tear the grounds up for a golf course. The beautiful gardens will be gone, and there will be no room for the flower show."

"Oh dear. That's a shame." Elspeth ruminated on this for a few seconds. "I suppose a lot of people are upset about that."

Violet snorted. "You can say that again. Adelaide is probably the most upset."

"Adelaide?"

"Adelaide Timmons. She runs the flower show. Lives down the street from you in Rose Cottage. You might have noticed the roses growing everywhere. Adelaide does love her flowers and roses especially."

"I did notice that cottage." Elspeth had a special interest in roses herself and had been admiring the cottage, which was three doors down and across the street from hers.

"You probably saw her running around here in her yellow wellies, shouting orders." Violet picked another shortbread off the tray. "She's done the show for decades. Practically lives for it, you know."

"You don't say. So, she'd be rather put off by the sale, then." Elspeth thought about the whispering voices she'd heard on the other side of the rose trellis. Had one of them been Adelaide?

"Indeed."

Elspeth shifted in her chair. "The victim... er... the man who died. Didn't he own Crowley Hall?"

Violet's gaze narrowed. "Yeah."

"Well, I just wondered, not knowing anything about your laws over here, but would his death affect the sale in any way?"

Violet chewed her shortbread thoughtfully. "I suppose it might. Depends on where they are in the sale process, I think. Someone would inherit the estate, and I'm not sure if they could be held to the sale."

"I suppose that *someone* would be his wife," Elspeth ventured.

Violet frowned. "Not sure about that. He had a daughter from a previous marriage. Lady Jane died when Angie—that's the daughter—was young. I guess it depends on what is in his will, though I have to say, if his death does nix the sale, there will be quite a few besides Adelaide who will be happy about that."

"Oh, really?" Elspeth leaned toward Violet, encouraging the woman to elaborate and not wanting to miss a word.

"Yes. The entire Village Protection Committee

would be delighted. We don't like to see things changed in the village."

"And who is on that committee?"

"Well, there's Adelaide, of course, and Edith Wilson, myself, and Judith Hastings. She's Sir John's sister..." Her eyes grew wide, and her hands flew to her cheeks. "Oh, dear, poor Judith. I wonder if she knows about John. She'll be terribly upset. He's her only living relative aside from her niece."

"Poor thing," Elspeth said soothingly, while she mentally added Adelaide, Violet, Edith Wilson, and Judith to her suspect list.

On the other side of the tea tent, Elspeth saw the woman from Thistle Cottage talking to a few people she recognized as villagers. Did she have a past association with the village, or was she simply chatting? Maybe she was just scoping out the pastry situation so she could tuck more of them away in her purse.

Now that Elspeth had more viable suspects, this strange lady wasn't as interesting. She wouldn't discount her completely, but Adelaide, Edith, and Judith were a lot more likely. And if one of them happened to own the threatening voice she'd heard early that morning, all the better.

First on her list was Adelaide Timmons. It appeared she had a lot to lose from the sale of Crowley

Hall if the flower show was so important to her. Elspeth had no idea what Adelaide looked like, but how hard could it be to find someone in yellow wellies, barking orders?

IDA MARCHED toward the orchid tent, a vanilla scone nestled inside a napkin in her purse. To her, the scone was more like a biscuit, short and round and not at all like the ones she got at home that came in a variety of flavors. Still, she did admit they were delicious. She'd regrettably left the clotted cream on the table—that wouldn't travel well in her purse, and investigating the murder took precedence.

Despite the disturbing events of the morning, Ida had been told the flower show would proceed as usual. Tickets had already been sold and vendors already set up, not to mention the money the floral exhibitors and contestants and the show itself had already outlaid. As she watched the police discreetly wheel the body away, taking care to stay behind the tents and away from the stream of attendees, she wondered if the murder might bring in even more visitors because people were always morbidly curious.

In the tea tent, Ida had spoken to some of the

villagers she'd become acquainted with. She'd hoped to get the inside scoop on the victim's relatives and was not disappointed. It seemed that Sir John had a much younger second wife, a disgruntled daughter, and a spinster sister who lived in a cottage on the property. Any one of them could have a motive for murder, but she couldn't exactly interrogate them, especially not so soon after the death. She'd have to find an excuse to talk to them and pretend she was giving condolences.

She'd gotten another lead, too, and that was where she was heading now. It seemed that there was another person who would benefit from Sir John's death. Kenneth Fairlane.

According to what she'd heard about Kenneth, the village resident had a long-standing competition with John for the orchid blue-ribbon prize. It was a friendly competition, or so they said, but John usually won. Maybe this year, Kenneth wanted the win. He was getting older, and it might be his last chance. Ida didn't think winning an orchid contest was worth killing over, but she'd seen stranger things.

The competition tent was a white-and-yellow-striped tent big enough to hold a circus in. It was set up with rows of tables, where the contestants were primping and preening their plants.

The entire tent was thick with foliage and flowers. Contestants misted their plants with small spritzers, their colorful gardening gloves caked with dirt. The humid air was spiced with the earthy scent of moist dirt and the perfume of flowers.

Ida stopped to admire some pansies, their colorful face-like petals smiling at her. Maybe she would set out some pots of pansies on her deck when she got home. The deck didn't get much sun, but she knew pansies liked shade.

Over in the right corner, she spotted the orchids. Dozens of delicate blooms atop tall, thin stems. The colors were awe-inspiring—vibrant blues and deep purples, and even the white ones seemed brighter than your average flower.

A white-haired man wearing gold wire-rimmed glasses bent over a pot containing a plant of velvety purple blooms. That must be Kenneth. Ida squared her shoulders and approached him.

"What lovely flowers. You sure have a green thumb for orchids." Ida wasn't above buttering up suspects to get them to open up to her.

Kenneth looked up and smiled. "Thank you. This one here is a relatively rare species."

"How fascinating. I'm glad you'll still have the

competition even with the... you know." Ida tilted her head in the general direction of the koi pond.

Kenneth frowned as he patted something that looked like large coffee grounds around the green-glazed pot housing the orchid. "Yes, dreadful business."

"Though I suppose it increases your chances of winning the orchid contest," Ida said innocently.

Kenneth's eyes jerked up to meet hers. "Well, I certainly don't want to win *that* way." He turned and opened a five-foot-tall plastic cupboard that stood behind him. Apparently it was some sort of storage or tool cupboard. Almost every table had one, and Ida figured they were brought in temporarily for the contestants to store their supplies. He pulled out a small pruning tool before quickly shutting the door.

"Of course not. It must be an awful feeling to have your rival gone like that. I'm sure you were on most friendly terms," Ida said.

Kenneth cleared his throat, squinting at a leaf on the plant and bringing the tool up toward it. "I don't know about that. He did grow nice orchids."

Ida decided to try another line of questioning. "I suppose you must get into the show pretty early in the morning to make sure your plants are perfectly pruned."

By Ida's estimation, Sir John was likely killed

before the show opened. He hadn't been dead long, but if the show had been open, there would have been too many people, and someone would have seen. That made Ida wonder about the murder weapon. From the glance she'd gotten at his head, it was something blunt and rather large like a rock or maybe a shovel or spade. Her eyes drifted to the cabinet behind Kenneth. Too bad those doors were closed.

"Not really," Kenneth said as he snipped a dying leaf off with precision. The leaf fluttered to the table, and he looked up at Ida. "I live next door to the hall, so I tend to my plants in my greenhouse and then bring them over. Of course, there is minor trimming that's done here, but I don't need to come in early."

Was it Ida's imagination, or had he put undue emphasis on the word *early*?

"Must be convenient to live right next door." Maybe not so much if he was now going to have a golf course and resort as a neighbor. "But it must be a chore to drag all your tools and plants with you."

Kenneth glanced at a rusty blue wheelbarrow that sat next to the cabinet. "I use the wheelbarrow. Lots of us do. Adelaide Timmons, who runs the place, is always going back and forth with hers."

"You must be very serious to have your own green-house." In her peripheral vision, Ida saw the plainclothes police approaching the tent. Shoot, they were heading this way. She'd better cut things short, as they'd already seen her dropping her rain bonnet at the crime scene, and she didn't want to blip onto their radar again. It was unfortunate because she felt like Kenneth was hiding something, and she would have liked more time to try to find out what that was. Maybe she could come back to him later.

"I guess you could say it's become a bit of an obsession." Kenneth shrugged. "But I'm an old man, and my opportunities are limited."

"Indeed. I know how that is." Ida edged away. "I'll let you get on with your pruning then. Good luck with the contest."

As Ida hurried down a side aisle in an attempt to avoid the police, she heard the cabinet open. She turned back to see Kenneth had both doors open wide. A quick survey of the contents told her there was no shovel or spade that could be the murder weapon. But Kenneth lived next door—could he have zipped home and hidden the murder weapon in his greenhouse? No one would think it was suspicious to see him carrying a shovel or spade, and he could have been lying about not being here early.

Though killing someone to win a contest seemed like a silly motive, Ida realized that Kenneth had not one but two motives. One was to win the contest, but the other might be more compelling—to make sure the sale of Crowley Hall didn't go through, so he wouldn't have to live next door to a noisy golf course and hotel.

CHAPTER 4

*I*t wasn't hard for Elspeth to find the woman with the yellow wellies. She was behind the potting tent, her boots marred with bark mulch and dirt, slinging sacks of loam like they were light as goose feathers. Elspeth admired her fortitude. The woman had to be nearing seventy.

"Bill, make sure you get some of the loam over to the geranium tent," she barked at the teenager who appeared to be helping her. "And don't forget to pick up any branches in the back near the forest. Throw them in the wheelbarrow here, and we'll send them through the wood chipper later tonight."

Elspeth was disappointed that the tone and inflection of the voice were not similar to those of the woman she'd heard on the path early that morning.

Then again, that didn't mean that Adelaide Timmons wasn't the killer or that the whispering woman *was* the killer, for that matter.

Adelaide grunted as she picked up another bag then paused when she saw Elspeth. "Oh, hello. Can I help you?" she asked in a pleasant manner.

"No… er… yes… I mean, I just wanted to tell you what a lovely flower show you've put on. You are Adelaide Timmons, aren't you?" Elspeth asked.

"I am." Adelaide pulled off her green gingham gardening glove and held out her hand. It was warm and calloused and covered in bandages, but her handshake was firm.

"It's a shame about the little *incident*," Elspeth said.

Adelaide frowned. "Yes. I suppose the show must go on, though we will miss John terribly, of course."

"You were friends?"

Adelaide put the glove back on and hefted another sack into the wheelbarrow. "We've both lived in the village a long time. John has been nice enough to let us use the grounds here for the flower show."

"Too bad this will be the last year."

Adelaide hesitated mid-toss. "Where did you hear that?"

"I have a keen interest in flowers and was

wondering about tickets for next year's show but was told there might not be one."

Adelaide sighed and tossed the bag then nodded to Bill to take the wheelbarrow away. She wiped her brow with the back of her wrist. Tossing bags was hard work. Sweat beaded on her lip, and her hair was damp around her face. "Unfortunately, that's true. But you never know. Maybe things will change."

Indeed, maybe they would. Especially if the sale couldn't go through because Sir John was dead.

"It must be hard work running this show. I bet you have to get in at the crack of dawn. It's too bad you didn't see anyone suspicious lurking about."

Wariness clouded Adelaide's gray eyes. "Maybe it was a good thing I didn't, or I might have been the next victim. As it is, I got in late this morning. Anyway, it's likely the killer ran off through the woods behind the koi pond. No one would have seen them."

Elspeth glanced in the direction of the pond. She couldn't see it from where they were, but the woods loomed at the edge of the show. It wasn't like there was a fence or anything to keep people out... or in, for that matter. "I suppose you're right."

"Even if I had been on time, I probably wouldn't have seen the killer." Adelaide gestured to the grounds. "The show covers an acre, and the odds of us running into each other are slim. The only person I saw for the first hour was Edith Wilson."

"Edith Wilson." Elspeth paused for a few seconds, pretending as if she were trying to remember who Edith Wilson was, when, in fact, the woman was at the forefront of her memory. "Oh yes, she's a member of the Village Protection Committee along with you, isn't she?"

"You seem to know an awful lot about our little village." Adelaide's tone bordered on suspicious.

Elspeth smiled her charming old-lady smile. "Of course. I make it my business to find out about the local villages I visit. I think it's charming that you want to protect the quaint village life."

The praise did its trick. Adelaide's shoulders relaxed. "Why, yes, we think so. It's important to keep up traditions, don't you think?"

Elspeth nodded. "Of course. The committee must be livid about the sale of Crowley Hall. That's going to change things quite a bit."

Adelaide glanced toward the mansion.

"Yes, it is," she said in a flat tone.

"Though now that Sir John is no longer alive, I suppose the sale will be caught up in red tape. It might even fall through. That could be good for the village and the flower show."

Adelaide's gaze jerked back to Elspeth, her eyes narrowed. "I really hadn't considered that. Why are you asking so many questions? It seems you are a bit more interested than warranted for an outsider, and I think you should—"

"Yes, why *are* you asking so many questions?"

Elspeth whirled around to see the police detectives standing behind her. The frumpy woman had a serious expression, and the young man wore one of curious amusement.

"I just have a natural curiosity is all. Not much to do at my age but think about things."

"You don't say." The woman stepped in her path blocking her from leaving. "Are you visiting? You don't sound like a local."

Elspeth offered her hand. She supposed it might be beneficial to make friends with the local police, then maybe she could wheedle some information out of them. "Elspeth Whipple. Visiting for the flower show."

"Detective Chief Inspector Louise James and Sergeant Maxwell Evans." They shook hands. The woman's handshake was firm, her eyes intelligent. Elspeth got the impression that she, DCI Louise James, was a lot smarter than she'd first appeared to be at the crime scene. The woman was not someone one should underestimate. "Did you know the deceased?"

"Oh no, not at all," Elspeth said. Was she a suspect? How interesting. If the police were considering her, that meant they had no good clues as to who had actually done it. "I just happened to be there when the body was found."

"Actually, you found the body, didn't you?" Sergeant Evans looked at his notes. "The description from a witness sounds like you."

Elspeth straightened. Surely they didn't think she'd put it there. "Sort of. A little girl pushed the lily pads away to see the fish, and I noticed something amiss in the depths of the pond."

"I hope finding a body didn't disturb you too much." DCI James's words sounded sympathetic, but her eyes gave Elspeth the impression that what she was thinking had nothing to do with feeling sorry for an old woman.

"Not at all. I'm a tough old bird. Now, I'll let you get on with your business." Elspeth hurried off before they could detain her. Suddenly she needed a soothing cup of tea.

DETECTIVE CHIEF INSPECTOR Louise James weaved between piles of bark mulch as she left the area where they'd been questioning Adelaide Timmons. Her suspect list was growing. Plenty of them had a motive, but still something about the case eluded her.

"She was rather tight lipped," Max Evans said.

"Aren't they all?" Louise and Max had done their share of investigations in tiny English villages, and it was always the same. Either they gave little information or what they did give was a lie.

"Secretive lot," Max said as they walked along a path lined with tall evergreen topiaries in enormous pots. "Too bad we haven't found the murder weapon. I didn't see anything among her tools that fit the bill."

"Me neither. We'll find it in due time. It must still be here somewhere. The victim hasn't been dead that long. But if it is a shovel or spade, we have our work cut out for us. The place is full of them."

Max nodded. "What do you make of the old ladies?"

So Max *had* noticed them. Louise felt a burst of pride almost as one would feel for a child. In a way, Max was like a child. Louise was almost old enough to be his mother, and she supposed she played a mentoring role in his police career. They'd been partnered for several years now, and he was turning out to be a fine cop.

Of course, Louise had noticed the old ladies right

away. Did they really think that trick of dropping something fooled her? She might have written that off as a coincidence if she hadn't found each of them talking to the suspects.

"They are definitely up to something. You know how inquisitive old ladies can be. Especially the ones visiting from the States. Seems they all think they are miniature Miss Marples. Probably from watching too many episodes of *Murder, She Wrote*." Louise stopped and waited for Max, who was marveling at a display of brilliant blue hydrangeas.

Max straightened. "I just hope they don't get in the way of the investigation."

Louise snorted. "They can hardly hurt. The villagers don't tell us anything anyway. The Miss Marples probably get more information out of them than we do."

"Isn't that always the way? Eager to talk to strangers, mistrustful of the law. But I know you can figure it out and get them to talk."

Louise's heart swelled with pride at Max's confidence in her. When they'd first been paired, he'd been a gung-ho rookie who was skeptical about taking orders from a woman who reminded him of his mother. Louise knew her appearance wasn't exactly that of a top-notch investigator. Because of that, she was often underestimated, a fact that, most times, she used to her advantage. She'd discovered early on that dressing frumpily and acting like she couldn't put two clues together loosened people's lips.

Max had caught on to this tactic early, and now they made an unbeatable team with the largest record in the district for closing cases. It was a blessing and a curse. Because of their high close rate, they were often assigned these twisty village murder cases.

"I'm sure I could get them to talk, but I bet those old ladies can get them to talk a lot more easily and a lot sooner, too." Louise glanced at Max out of the corner of her eye.

Max returned her gaze, a slight frown forming between his dark brows. "What are you proposing?"

Louise shrugged. "If my guess about them fancying themselves to be investigators is correct, we might be able to use that to our advantage."

"What do you mean, like deputize them or something? I don't think that's done anymore. Maybe in the olden days when you were a rookie with the Bow Street Runners but not now." Max gave her a good-natured jab.

"Very funny. I don't mean to let them know we want them to help us. That might go to their heads," Louise said. "But what if we could use their natural inquisitive nature to get them to ask the right questions to the right people?"

"Sounds like that could get dangerous."

"We wouldn't want that." Louise would never put a citizen in danger, but she'd been a cop for a long time and knew what would and would not constitute danger. "We'd keep a close eye on them to make sure they're safe."

"I doubt the old ladies are going to just fall in line with your plan. They're probably already bored with the whole thing."

Louise didn't think so. She'd sized them up at the koi pond and knew their type. Intelligent and persistent. The type that didn't let go once they had something on their minds, and the two of them definitely had this investigation on their minds. They were the types that would ask the questions in a clever way, too, so as to get the information they needed without the suspects even knowing it was happening.

"Oh, I think they will. Bet on it?" Louise and Max often had friendly side bets on aspects of their cases. Louise usually won, and she knew she was right this time.

Max's pace slowed, and he turned to her. "What's the bet?"

"Lunch. If they fall for my plan, you buy. Otherwise, I will."

Max stopped and thrust out his hand. "Okay, deal."

They shook hands then continued along the path.

"So how would this work? We give them a few clues then follow them and listen in when they talk to people?" Max asked.

"Something like that. They seem like smart ladies. We already know they've figured out two of the suspects and questioned them already. Maybe we could have a talk with them and drop a few hints about some of the other suspects and see what happens."

"You'll play the dumb, frumpy detective again, I assume." Max knew how much Louise loved playing dumb.

"Of course. I don't think the two ladies know each other, but I think it's better if we bring them together. Safer that way, and we won't have to rely on just one account of whatever they dig up from the locals."

"Well, I suppose it can't hurt as long as we keep them safe. But where do you think we would find these little Miss Marples?"

Louise wasn't a top detective for nothing. She knew exactly where to find them. "Where all old ladies go after interrogating a suspect. The tea tent."

CHAPTER 5

Ida plopped a fluffy dollop of clotted cream on her scone and sat back in the folding metal chair as she ate it. The pastry was delicious, though she had to admit the name "clotted cream" had put her off. It sounded disgusting. But when she discovered, on her second day here, that it was simply cream that had been cooked, she tried it and never looked back.

As she took a sip of bergamot tea, she surveyed the tea tent. Of course that strange woman from Hyacinth Cottage was here, seated only a few tables away. Ida wondered how that woman had known the body was in the koi pond. Was it merely a coincidence, and if so, then why did she linger at the scene when the police came?

But there were so many more interesting suspects. Family members, the entire Village Protection Committee, and of course, Kenneth Fairlane. If only Ida knew what the murder weapon was, she could look in that little cabinet of his. Was there a way she could wheedle that information out of the police?

Just as she had that thought, the police appeared at the edge of the tent. Ida almost dropped her tea. They were scanning the crowd, and the gaze of the frumpy woman came to rest on her!

Her nerves jangled as they made their way into the tent. Surely they weren't coming for her... No, fortunately, they were making a beeline toward the Hyacinth Cottage woman. Aha! Ida's instincts had been correct—the woman *was* a suspect!

Ida took another bite of the scone, adding extra clotted cream as a reward for being correct about the woman. The detective was helping her stand. Were they leading her off to jail right now? But, instead of heading out of the tent, they turned and started making their way further into the tent.

Oh dear, they were heading straight for Ida!

"Good day, ma'am," the young male detective addressed Ida as they approached her table.

"Good day." Ida eyed the group with suspicion. The Hyacinth Cottage woman looked as suspicious and surprised as Ida, which was a relief. For a minute, Ida had thought that maybe the other woman had *brought* the police to her, but now it seemed to be the other way around. But why?

"Sorry for the intrusion," the frumpy female detective said. "We are making some routine inquiries, and we happened to notice the two of you at the koi pond. We thought it might save time to ask the questions of you together."

The other woman frowned at Ida, and Ida frowned back while addressing the detective. "I suppose that could work."

"Very good." The policewoman took a wallet from the pocket of her trench coat and flipped it open to reveal a badge. "I'm Detective Chief Inspector Louise James, and this is Sargent Maxwell Evans."

"Nice to meet you." Ida shook hands with both of them, then her gaze came to rest on the other woman.

"Oh, this is Elspeth Whipple," DCI James said. "You two don't know each other?"

"No." Ida shook hands with the other woman, thinking what an odd name Elspeth was. "Nice to meet you."

"And you." Elspeth's handshake was firm, and Ida saw a friendly curiosity in her cornflower-blue eyes. Perhaps the woman wasn't so bad after all.

"You're staying in Hyacinth Cottage, aren't you?" Ida asked.

Elspeth nodded. "And you're in Thistle?"

"Yes, right next door. Won't you sit down?" Ida gestured to the seats, and DCI James practically shoved Elspeth into one of them.

"We'll stand, but Ms. Whipple doesn't need to. We have only a few questions." DCI James nodded to Evans, and he whipped out a notepad. "Now, where are you both from?"

"Mystic Notch, New Hampshire," Elspeth said.

"Brooke Ridge Falls, New Hampshire," Ida said, practically at the same time.

Both women glanced at each other. They were from the same state? Ida felt an unwanted bond starting to form between them.

"Are we suspects?" Elspeth asked, echoing Ida's thoughts and earning another notch of approval. Ida slid her plate of scones over to the other woman and indicated for her to help herself.

"No, but you were both at the scene where the body was found, and I have a feeling you are both very observant." DCI James smiled at them, and Ida found new respect for her. She wasn't as dumb as Ida thought if she'd noticed how observant she was. "So did either of you see anything suspicious?"

"Other than a body in a koi pond?" Ida glanced at Elspeth. "I didn't really notice anything."

Elspeth shook her head. "Me neither."

"Did you hear anything or see anyone suspicious that morning?"

Ida looked down at her scone. Should she tell them about her suspects? Surely they already had the family members on their list, but did they know about the Village Protection Committee? They'd been to talk to Kenneth Fairlane, so they knew about him. They might be smarter than she thought, but that was still no reason to spill her guts about every suspicion. And what if she were wrong? She wouldn't want to get someone in trouble with the police for no reason.

"No," Elspeth and Ida said at the same time.

"You didn't see a tall, thin woman in her late twenties with paint on her?" DCI James asked.

Ida's suspect radar went into the red. The description was very specific, so the police must have a reason to suspect this woman. "With paint on her? I don't think so."

"Do you think she's the killer?" Elspeth's eyes gleamed with interest, and Ida felt a kindred spirit in the other woman. Clearly she had a fondness for solving murders the same as Ida. Perhaps being in the cottage next to hers would come in handy… other than all the cats, that is.

"She's the victim's daughter, Angie Hastings," DCI James said. Sergeant Evans gave her a reprimanding look, and her expression turned guarded.

"A suspect?" Elspeth asked.

"Er… no. I mean, she's just here at the show." DCI James sounded like she was trying to cover up, and Ida mentally moved Angie to the top of her suspect list.

"If she's the daughter, wouldn't she inherit something? That's usually a motive," Ida pointed out.

"We really couldn't say." DCI James looked as if she wished she hadn't mentioned Angie. Or did she? Ida sensed a hint of satisfaction behind James's regretful expression.

"I don't remember any woman with paint. You say she's here at the flower show? Why is she covered in paint?" Elspeth asked.

"She's an artist, exhibiting her art in the vendors' tents." Sergeant Evans nodded his head in the direction of a cluster of tents. "Funny thing, she still seems to be carrying on as usual despite the grim news of her father's death."

Both Ida and Elspeth jerked their heads in the direction Sergeant Evans had indicated. Carrying on as normal even after her father's death? That was suspicious behavior right there. Ida figured that would be her next stop. She suspected that Elspeth was thinking the same thing. Now if the police would just leave and let her get on with it...

Movement outside the tent caught her eye. A uniformed policeman was lurking with a large implement in his hand. DCI James turned, and he signaled to her. She motioned him over, and he came to the table, glancing at Elspeth and Ida uncertainly.

"Found the murder weapon in the koi pond, or at least part of it," he said. "Just like you suspected."

Ida shoved the rest of her scone in her mouth, on full alert now.

DCI James looked flustered. "It was just a lucky guess. Honestly, I'm glad we didn't have to look too hard." She glanced at Ida and Elspeth.

"Officer Grantham has it." The uniform pointed to the side of the tent where another uniformed officer was holding half a spade wrapped in clear plastic. It was the bottom half, but the shaft was splintered and broken. The metal spade was rusty, and Ida couldn't make out if there was blood on it. Ida smiled with satisfaction. That was exactly what she'd thought the weapon was.

DCI James smiled at them. "Well, looks like we better get back to work. Let me buy you some tea for allowing us to take up your time." She signaled the wait staff.

Ida pushed out of her chair. "You don't need to do that. I really must be going."

DCI James put a firm hand on Ida's shoulder and pushed her back down in a rather forceful manner. Apparently the woman really wanted them to have some tea.

"I insist," Louise said as the waitress poured some masala chai into their cups. "We've taken up your time, and I appreciate you talking to us. I hope this whole matter isn't too disturbing for you."

"Oh no, not at all," Elspeth said.

"Nope, happens all the time back home." Ida ignored DCI James's curious look, her gaze focused on the spade. Where was the other half? Surely the police had looked over the entire pond for it. It wouldn't be hard to find if it were in there, which meant it wasn't. The killer must have kept it. That was good. It would make her job easier—find the top of the spade, and they'd have their killer. Now if she only knew where to look for it.

She sighed, took a sip of tea, her gaze meeting Elspeth's over the rim of her teacup.

ELSPETH PEERED over the rim of her teacup and assessed the woman who sat across the table from her. Ida's blue eyes twinkled with mischief, and Elspeth amended her previous suspicion that the woman might be involved in the murder. Clearly the woman was interested in solving the murder, just like she was.

And was it a coincidence that they were both from New Hampshire? Perhaps this was a sign. It sounded like Ida had already been forming some opinions on the case. Judging by the way Ida had been studying the murder weapon and how she'd wanted to rush off (presumably to find this Angie person, because that was exactly what Elspeth was going to do next), she was doing some investigating of her own. Why not join forces? Two minds were always better than one, and it was fun to have someone else to hash out ideas with.

Elspeth closed her eyes and asked her inner spirit for guidance. When she opened her eyes, they fell on a snow-white cat who sat at the very edge of the tent, staring at her with unblinking sky-blue eyes. Guess that was a sign. She turned her attention to Ida. With the detectives gone, now they could really talk.

"What do you make of that murder weapon?"

Ida picked another scone from the plate. Elspeth hoped she wasn't about to wrap it in a napkin and put it in her purse. She really should talk to the woman about that strange habit. Maybe when she knew her better.

"I knew it had to be something large and blunt. Looks like it was old and must have broken when the killer clonked Sir John over the head. I wonder why the killer kept the handle, though," Ida said.

"I bet it's so the police couldn't find fingerprints or DNA on it." Elspeth took a scone and daubed some clotted cream on it, noting the approval in the other woman's eyes. Ida had been testing her to see if she was up to snuff. She must have the same idea about teaming up.

Ida leaned forward, apparently satisfied with Elspeth's answer. "That's what I thought too. We'll have to make sure to check out all the suspect's gardening tools in case they haven't disposed of it already."

"Indeed." Elspeth said. "You've already talked to some of them?"

Ida took another sip of tea, apparently mulling over whether or not she should take Elspeth into her confidence. Finally she nodded and said, "Yes. Kenneth Fairlane."

"He would benefit from Sir John's death because

they were competitors for the orchid contest," Elspeth supplied.

"Yes!" Ida seemed excited that they were on the same wavelength.

"What did you find out?"

Ida's excitement evaporated. "Not much. He did have some tools locked in a cabinet, but I don't recall seeing a spade. He claims he wasn't here before the show opened. He lives next door and brings things from his greenhouse."

"Next door? To Crowley Hall?" Elspeth pressed her lips together. "I bet he wouldn't like the idea of the hall being made into a golf course."

"Exactly what I thought. I felt like he was hiding something—kept glancing at his wheelbarrow—but there are so many suspects."

"I agree," Elspeth said. "There's the family who might gain monetarily or might want to do away with Sir John to make sure he doesn't change the will. And then there is a committee dedicated to protecting the village. They probably wouldn't like the idea of a golf course being built either, and there is some question as to whether that sale will go through with Sir John no longer alive."

"And don't forget the woman that runs the flower

show. Adelaide Timmons. Apparently she lives for this show."

"I've already questioned her," Elspeth said proudly.

"You have? What did you discover?"

"Well, she's a hard worker," Elspeth said.

"I bet she's the type that shows up early every morning, then."

"She is but not this morning. This morning she was running late."

Ida's left brow quirked up, and she shoved the last of her scone in her mouth.

"I know, I know. Naturally she would say that if she were the killer and trying to pretend like she wasn't here, but she has a witness who saw her coming in late."

"Anyone we can talk to?"

Elspeth nodded. "A member of the Village Protection Committee, Edith Wilson."

"She's already on my list, so we can kill two birds with one stone." Ida frowned, and her gaze drifted over Elspeth's shoulder. She turned to see the white cat still lurking around the edge of the tent, watching them. "Um... this morning, you didn't happen to overhear something on the path behind our cottages, did you?"

"As a matter of fact, I did." Elspeth leaned across

the table and lowered her voice. "An argument of sorts."

Ida nodded enthusiastically. "And the woman sounded quite... desperate. Threatening, even."

"She did." Elspeth cocked her head as if trying to recall what she'd heard. "I believe her words were something about how village life would change over *her* dead body. Not over Sir John's, though."

Ida shrugged. "Semantics. She said she'd *fixed things* so village life would remain the same, didn't she?"

"That's correct," Elspeth said. "And that was early in the morning, perhaps around the time Sir John was killed."

"And wouldn't you say that selling Crowley Hall would disturb the village life?"

"Yes, I would."

"And the death of Sir John might ensure that the hall is not sold."

"We don't know that yet, but it's a safe assumption for us to go on for now."

Ida nodded. "Have you recognized that voice in anyone here?"

"No. It wasn't Adelaide Timmons. But we haven't met all the suspects yet."

Ida's intelligent eyes sparkled, and she said, "Then there seems to be only one course of action now."

Elspeth patted her lips with the napkin, tossed it on the table, and rose from her seat. Across the table, Ida did the same.

"I have a hankering to go view some art, don't you?" Elspeth asked.

"Indeed I do, and I believe the artisan tents are right down that path over there."

CHAPTER 6

*A*ngie Hastings's tent wasn't hard to find since all the tents had the names of the artists clearly marked. The artists' tents were situated in a ring around a small pond with a fountain in the middle. Impatiens, lilies, and other flowers ringed the pond, and Ida wondered whether they'd been planted for the flower show or if it had always been this lovely.

Ida cast a trepid eye at the pond. She hoped fish were all that was in there. Though she loved investigating, she didn't relish finding another body, at least not today.

Inside Angie's tent, the pungent smell of turpentine overpowered the lingering scent of flowers as Ida inspected the splashes and blobs of paint decorating the canvases hanging on all sides. Angie's style was modern, colorful blobs. Giant splotches of reds, yellows, and blues dominated. It wasn't exactly Ida's style, but judging by the high price tag, people must have liked it.

Angie Hastings was a tall, thin woman in her late twenties. Unruly dark hair dotted with yellow paint curled around her head. In fact, her whole body was covered in paint, and it was no wonder, Ida thought, as she watched her load up a brush and then whip it toward the canvas. Paint flew off and landed in a spray. Red dots that reminded her of blood.

She glanced at Elspeth and figured the other woman had the same opinion of Angie's artistic style, if the way her lips were pursed together was any indication. Be that as it may, they needed to strike up a conversation with her, and the best way Ida knew how to do that was to feign interest in the work and get her talking about herself.

"My, these paintings certainly are interesting." Ida turned to Elspeth. "Don't you think so?"

"Yes, indeed. The bright colors are so... um... bright!" Elspeth chirped.

Angie hurled another blob of paint at the canvas.

Splat! It landed in the center, creating a cobalt-blue amoeba shape.

Ida moved to stand next to her, looking at the

canvas and putting on her best art-admiring expression, with her index finger and thumb holding her chin. "What an interesting method. Are all your works done in this way, or are you particularly angry or upset today?"

Angie glanced at her. "I always work like this. Are you art lovers?"

"Yes, we are," Ida said.

"Especially... um... colorful and bright art," Elspeth added.

Angie dipped the brush into a blob of bright blue paint. Beside her was a table littered with enormous tubes of paint, rags, and paint thinner. A pile of business cards was stacked on the edge. Ida picked up one of the cards.

"Angie Hastings." She turned to Elspeth. "Hastings. Now why is that name familiar?"

Elspeth made a show of tilting her head and frowning as if trying to recall. "Wasn't that the name of the man that met with the, er... accident... this morning?"

Thwack!

Angie's paint missed the canvas, catching only the bottom and dripping down all over the easel.

Ida raised a brow at Elspeth as she asked Angie, "Are you any relation?"

Angie didn't look at her, just grabbed a rag and started cleaning the easel. "He was my father."

"Oh dear. I'm so sorry for your loss. Well, no wonder you are flinging the paint in such an angry manner."

Angie twisted the rag in her hand. "Thank you. It was a shock, but Father and I weren't close, so…"

"Of course, we understand," Elspeth said soothingly. "You're throwing yourself into your work."

"I admire your courage to go on," Ida said in an attempt to butter her up and win her confidence. "Losing a parent is a hard thing, but at least there is a silver lining."

"There is?" Angie frowned at her.

Ida nodded. "Especially for a starving artist. An inheritance is a great way to provide the necessities of life so you can pursue your passion."

"Inheritance?" Angie scowled. "I don't know about that. Dad had a new wife that I'm sure he'll leave everything to, and he didn't approve of my lifestyle."

"Surely your father wouldn't leave you out of his will," Elspeth said.

Angie picked up a tube of red paint and squeezed a blob of it onto her palette. "I don't know anything about a will."

"Because you weren't on good terms?" Ida asked.

"Dad thought I should be like him. Work on investments. Have a big mansion." Angie waved her hand in the direction of Crowley Hall, and Ida and Elspeth dodged the flecks of paint that splattered off the brush in every direction.

"That's a shame, especially now." Ida said "Still, I doubt a parent would leave his only child out of his will in favor of a new wife, even if he didn't approve of what you chose to do for a living."

Angie snorted then picked up a brush and loaded it with red paint. Her hands were covered in paint of all colors, but the red stood out to Ida, who, with her overactive imagination, pictured it as being blood.

"You haven't seen the new wife. About half his age. I can only think of one reason she'd want to marry an old grouch like my father. Do you know she talked him into selling the hall? Wanted to travel."

Ida saw the perfect opening to dig into a motive. "Did that upset you? I mean, the hall has been in your family for generations, right?"

"Yeah. But I don't really care about owning a big, old, moldy mansion. Too much work to take care of." Angie flicked the brush at the canvas, and tiny dots appeared.

"I heard the sale might be held up now that your father is dead," Elspeth chimed in.

"That will probably affect Celia more than anyone. I think she wanted to make sure that money was in the bank and not in the property. The traveling was just an excuse." Angie's face darkened, and she flicked the brush with such force that it created a big, red starburst on the canvas. "I doubt Celia cared about the house. The only one who will really be upset if it's sold is Aunt Judith."

"Aunt Judith?" Ida asked. Wasn't a Judith Hastings part of the Village Preservation Committee?

"Yeah, funny thing—she was just asking about the hall the other day. She lives in the caretaker's cottage and will have to vacate. Though Dad was giving her a nice sum of money to buy a modern place, she still loves that old hall." The corners of Angie's lips quirked up in a smile, apparently at fond thoughts of Aunt Judith. "Anyway, I told her if I ever inherited it, I'd just give the darn thing to her."

"That's very nice of you," Elspeth said as she inspected a splotchy painting.

Angie shrugged. "She's been a big supporter of my work, and like I said, I don't want the old place. But it's a moot point, right? Even if the sale is held up because of my father's death, I'm sure Celia will end up with it, and I bet she can't wait to dump the thing."

"Well, I guess since you have no interest, that won't

bother you." Elspeth had turned from her study of the painting and now appeared to be studying Angie.

"Not in the least. Unlike Aunt Judith, I don't have fond childhood memories of the place." Angie looked up from her work. "Judith really loves Crowley Hall. And this flower show. She spends hours manning the butterfly tent every year. I think it's the one thing she looks forward to."

"Butterfly tent?" Elspeth looked at Ida and edged her way out of the tent. "Why, that sounds lovely. What do you say, Ida? Should we go check it out?"

"I think so. We'll leave this nice young lady to her work. And do accept our condolences for the death of your father." Ida started out of the tent then paused and turned back to Angie. "It's too bad you weren't on better terms with your father. I mean, with the two of you here at the show this morning, if you'd been with him, the killer might not have been successful."

Angie looked up at her, pain etched across her face. "I suppose that's true. But even if we were on good terms, I wasn't here this morning, so I doubt that would have helped."

"Oh no?" Elspeth asked. "That's a shame. Where were you?"

Angie's eyes narrowed. "You sound like the police. I had some business to tend to down in the village." She turned back to her work, and Ida sensed they'd be getting no more information from her today.

"Well then, carry on with your work," Ida said cheerily.

Angie merely grunted and loaded her brush up with paint as the two ladies hurried off to their next destination.

CHAPTER 7

*E*lspeth leaned over and talked to Ida in a hushed tone as they traversed one of the many plant-laden paths that wound around the flower show. "Judith Hastings is a member of the Village Protection Committee."

"Isn't that interesting." Ida slowed in front of a display of begonias. "So she would have a lot of reasons to want to stop the sale of Crowley Hall."

"Old family home, would ruin the village, she'd have to find a new place to live." Elspeth ticked the reasons off on her fingers.

"I wonder if her voice will sound familiar to us."

"Someone's has to. Though it was in a whisper, so maybe we won't be able to recognize it?"

"I say we talk to all the members of this Village

Protection Committee. Do you know who the members are?"

"Yes. There's Violet Crosby, who I talked to in the tea tent, then Adelaide Timmons, Edith Wilson, and Judith Hastings." Elspeth thought she saw a familiar trench coat out of the corner of her eye, but when she looked back, she didn't see anyone. "Did you see those two police officers over there?"

Ida looked in the direction Elspeth indicated and shook her head. "No. Do you think they are following us? Surely they don't suspect us of something."

"Probably just my imagination. Anyway, I've talked to Violet and Adelaide and their voices were not familiar. I guess we'll soon find out about Judith."

Elspeth stopped in front of a large rose display. Back home, the vibrant display of roses that twined along the front porch of her Victorian home were the envy of Mystic Notch. The roses bloomed well into the fall, and people were always asking how she got so many blooms and how they lasted so long. Elspeth always smiled and said she used good fertilizer, but the truth was that, like many things in Mystic Notch, the roses had a little bit of magical help.

Elspeth was always looking for new rose varieties for her garden. She bent down to inspect a bright orange-and-yellow heirloom rosebush called Oranges 'n' Lemons. Such an unusual color, and it would look lovely in the side garden. Next to it, a hybrid tea rose plant in dark red with outer petals that were almost black caught her eye. Beyond that, a gorgeous climbing rose with an abundance of delicate petals shaded light pink on the inside and white on the outside climbed up a trellis.

There were roses of all colors—white, pink, red, yellow. Shrubs, vines, and even tree roses, which were really just a rosebush that was pruned and trained to grow its blooms at the top like a tree.

Ida leaned over and sniffed a pale-yellow English rose that was in full bloom. "Roses are lovely, but the smell isn't all that strong. I prefer lilacs or lily of the valley."

"For a flowery scent, those can't be beat," Elspeth said as she broke away from the roses and started back down the path. "I think I see the butterfly tent over there."

The butterfly tent was enclosed in netting. Inside were plants both short and tall. Shrubs, flowers, and butterfly bushes with large, purple cones of flowers. Elspeth moved the netting aside as instructed by the placard next to it, and they stepped inside quickly so as not to let any of the butterflies out.

A family with two young children ran in front of

them, the children chasing a bright orange-and-black monarch butterfly. Two women were huddled in the corner, heads bent together. Elspeth recognized one of them.

"That's Violet Crosby, one of the members of the Village Protection Committee," she whispered to Ida.

"The other one must be Judith." Ida started toward them.

The two women were talking in hushed tones, but Elspeth could just hear the woman she assumed was Judith say, "...And we ran into Edith. She'd talked Shirley into opening the town hall so she could get a development plans for the Crowley Ha—"

Violet noticed them approaching, and Judith cut off her sentence as the two women stepped apart. Violet cleared her throat, recognition flickering across her face as she looked at Elspeth.

"Hello there!" Elspeth said. "Nice to see you again. Violet, was it?"

"Yes... Oh, I do remember now. You're Elspeth from the tea tent?" The woman's smile seemed a bit fake and laced with suspicion. Her eyes were a bit too narrow, the corners of her mouth not quite turned up enough.

"Yes. That's right." Elspeth turned inquisitive eyes on the other woman in the hopes of an introduction.

"This is Judith Hastings." Violet gestured toward the woman who was about in her mid-sixties. She was tall with gray curly hair cut in a shoulder-length bob. Her eyes were red-rimmed—no surprise since she'd just lost her brother that morning. Seemed odd if she were upset that she would still be manning the tent, but if Elspeth had learned anything in this little village it was that the show must go on.

Violet was looking at Ida expectantly, and Elspeth introduced her, and everyone shook hands.

"Well, I must be going." Violet exchanged a sly look with Judith then turned to Elspeth and Ida. "Enjoy the butterflies!"

"Welcome to the butterfly tent." Judith gestured to the area, her voice a bit too cheery for someone whose brother had just been murdered. Then again, Elspeth could see a hint of grief in her gray eyes. She glanced at Ida who had her ear cocked toward the woman. Judith's voice was not the one they'd heard on the path.

"We have all species of butterflies here. Monarch, swallowtail, peacock, tortoiseshell, and even a rare blue morpho," Judith indicated a butterfly that had landed on a leaf, its iridescent blue wings lazily opening and closing.

"They certainly are pretty," Elspeth said.

"And friendly." Ida ducked to avoid a yellow swallowtail that had been aiming for the top of her head.

Judith laughed. "Indeed they are! Why, they'll come and land right on you if you stand still enough."

Elspeth stood still, holding her arm out. A small, silvery-white butterfly with dark dots on its wings drifted over and landed on her bare arm, its touch light as a feather.

"We have butterflies in all states here. Some are in their cocoon." Judith gestured to a bush that had an ugly brown cocoon suspended from the bottom of a leaf. "And some are still caterpillars." She turned to gesture toward a fat, striped caterpillar on a leaf.

"All phases of life and death," Ida said. She really knew how to set the conversation up to go in the desired direction.

Not wanting to miss the opportunity Ida had provided, Elspeth plastered on her most sympathetic face and said, "Speaking of death, I believe condolences are in order."

Judith blinked, looking startled. "Oh, you mean my brother. Thanks so much." She looked away, her voice softening. "We were close as children but not so much now. Still, it's a blow."

"I hear you live here on the estate. Wasn't he a big part of your life?" Ida asked.

Judith scowled. "I live in the caretaker's cottage. It wasn't like I lived in the house with him. Not that I would want to with that new wife. Still, it's the only home I've ever known."

"Then you must be terribly upset to have to move." Elspeth spied a flutter of tan just outside the tent. Was that the woman detective? She craned her neck to see, but no one was there.

"How did you know about that?" Judith's voice was laced with suspicion.

"It's hardly a secret," Ida said as a peacock butterfly, its colorful spots standing out against its plain brown wings, landed on top of her snow-white coif. Her eyes angled upward as if searching for it. "The whole village is abuzz about the sale."

"I suppose it is. Yes, it is a disappointment to have to move."

"Maybe now that your brother can't go through with the sale, the hall will fall to you?" Elspeth ventured.

Judith shook her head. "Doubtful. I believe it would go to my niece, Angie, but it depends on John's will." She drew in a deep breath.

"Of course. We don't know how those things work over here," Elspeth said, hoping that she would keep talking and enlighten them as to what she knew about the will.

"Same as for you, I suppose. Oh, of course we have all the family lineage stuff and so on, which used to be more formal back in the day. These days, inheritances are more modern. Though Celia has been hinting that there will be a big change to the family, so who knows what will happen."

"A change? Well, John was selling the hall to travel, so that would be a big change." Elspeth wondered if that was it, though. The sale was not a secret, so why would Celia have to hint?

Judith pressed her lips together. "I suppose that could be it, but she had a glint in her eye that tells me something else was afoot."

"Surely you don't suspect..." Ida let her voice drift off with the insinuation.

Judith watched a small brown-and-orange butterfly flit from one flower to another. "Who knows what she would do. She doesn't seem that upset. Oh, she's putting on a good show and all. Turning on the waterworks and vowing to enter John's orchids in the contest so he can win posthumously. If you ask me, she's only interested in hanging around the judging tents so she can see Derek."

Ida and Elspeth exchanged a glance. Elspeth had

been worried that she wouldn't be able to get any information out of Judith, but the woman was spilling her guts like she'd guzzled down one of the special teas Pepper St. Onge made back in Mystic Notch.

"And just who is Derek?" Ida asked.

Judith jerked her attention from the butterfly to Ida. "Oh dear, now listen to me prattling on. I really shouldn't be talking out of school. Derek is some sort of natural healer. You've probably seen him around, waving his hands over the flowers. If you ask me, that's all bunk." She made a face expressing her opinion of natural healers. "But Mrs. Crosby certainly believes in it. She has him come in before the show opens every morning to give her prize petunias special spiritual vibes."

Interesting.

"So Derek was here early this morning?" Elspeth asked.

Judith nodded. "Oh yes, I saw him myself. Violet is very determined to have the most vibrant petunias."

"So then you were here early too?" Ida asked.

"This morning? Oh, no, actually, I got here only a few minutes before the show started, but Derek was already well into his routine." Judith lightly stroked the wings of a monarch that had landed on a nearby trumpet vine with the tip of her finger.

Elspeth glanced down at the woman's shoes. She had on canvas sneakers with a water stain covering three-quarters of the tips. Of course, that could have happened anywhere. This was a plant show, and things were constantly being watered, and Elspeth's shoes had a water line from the dew-soaked grass. But still... a splash from throwing something in the koi pond would have done that too. Except John was likely killed an hour or so before the show opened, and Judith had said she wasn't here, though Elspeth sensed she was being evasive about that.

"Did you see or hear anything unusual?" Elspeth asked. "The koi pond isn't too far from here..."

"I should say not!" Judith looked affronted. "If I'd known what was going on there, I would certainly have stopped it." Her eyes narrowed. "You ladies ask an awful lot of questions. Maybe you should leave."

Just then, Ida's stomach growled. "That's not a bad idea. I'm starving. What do you say we grab some lunch, and then afterwards we can interrogate the rest of the... er... I mean, check out the rest of the show."

"Good idea." Elspeth followed Ida out of the tent. She could feel Judith's narrow-eyed glare all the way out.

CHAPTER 8

*D*CI Louise James ducked behind a tall arborvitae in a gigantic pot. "I told you those ladies would be able to get the locals to talk."

Max shook his head. "Judith blabbed on like she was on a lie detector. Maybe we should hire some old ladies to work on the police force."

Louise snorted. "Don't mention that to our little Marples. They'd probably jump at the chance." She peeked around the tree to see where the ladies were going next. Her guess was they would try to talk to Derek or Celia, but it looked like they were heading for the exit.

Max slipped out from behind the adjoining tree and started down the path, darting from shrub to tree and keeping far back so they wouldn't notice him. Not that noticing them was likely with the way the two ladies had their heads bent together.

Louise smiled to herself. She was pleased that the amateur interrogators had provided them with more information than they could get on their own, but what made her even happier was that it appeared that she'd inadvertently started a friendship in bringing them together.

"So maybe those rumors we've heard about Celia Hastings and Derek Keswick are true," Max said.

"If Judith can be believed. Sounded a bit like sour grapes." Louise ducked behind a topiary as Ida stopped and glanced behind her. "We should see what they've got for garden tools, though."

"Yeah, too bad there were no fingerprints or DNA found on the murder weapon."

"Likely on the handle, and since it hasn't turned up in any dumpsters or landfills, my guess is the killer has it stashed somewhere."

"At least the information the old ladies gleaned corroborated our suspicions. They sure do have a way of getting people to talk." Max craned his neck to see above the crowd. "I think they're leaving."

"Probably going for lunch," Louise said. "Did you hear that sassy one's stomach growling? I've seen the way she puts away those scones and seed cakes. Even stashes them in her purse. For a thin little thing, she sure doesn't like to be too far from food."

"Neither do I." Max looked at his watch pointedly.

"Right, well, seems like they are going back to their cottages. They'll be safe there, so let's say we go to lunch ourselves. You're buying."

"I am?"

"Yeah, you lost the bet. Those little amateur detectives are proving to be worth their weight in gold. Let's hurry it up. I think I know where they're going after lunch, and I want to be in position before they get there, just in case."

"WE HAVE lots of suspects but no solid evidence," Ida said as she opened the door to Thistle Cottage.

They'd decided to take lunch back at her cottage so they could have a private place to go over the clues. Plus, she had a whole container of egg salad and homemade bread she'd bought at the bakery in the village, and she wanted to use it up. One could only eat so much egg salad by themselves.

"This looks similar to my cottage." Elspeth wandered over to the French doors that led to the patio. "Don't you love how the patios are decorated with such lush greenery and flowers?"

"Yes, it's very lovely." Ida put the egg salad and some bread on the counter then proceeded to make sandwiches.

"Can I help you with anything?" Elspeth asked.

"Oh, no, there's not much to do." Ida appreciated the offer, but the kitchen area was tiny, and she didn't like anyone getting in her way. "We could eat outside if you like."

"That would be nice." Elspeth glanced at the latch to the French doors.

"You go ahead, and I'll bring the sandwiches out. Would you like lemonade to drink?"

"That would hit the spot." Elspeth opened the door and went out to the patio.

Ida finished up the sandwiches and put them on little china plates then balanced them on a tole tray along with two glasses and the pitcher of lemonade.

As Ida joined Elspeth at the wrought-iron table in the garden, her eye was drawn to the brick wall at the end of the patio. "We still haven't determined whose voice it was that we heard on the path this morning."

"I know. We have one more member of the Village Protection Committee to talk to. Edith Wilson. Even if it is her, though, there's no guarantee the person we heard is the killer."

"No, but the timing is right. That was just under an hour before the show opened, wasn't it?" Ida took a bite of her sandwich.

"Yes, and Sir John was likely killed a bit before that. The path does go all around the village, so I suppose that person could have killed him at the koi pond then escaped through the woods."

Ida nodded. "I'm sure the killer escaped down that path in the woods. Why would they go all the way through the show? Less chance of being seen in the woods."

"Unless they were trying to be seen, to make it look like they hadn't just killed someone," Elspeth said.

"Good point."

Elspeth picked up her sandwich and looked it over as if she moonlighted as a health inspector. "This bread wasn't in your purse, was it?"

"No." Ida blushed. Elspeth must have seen her putting scones in her purse at some point. It was a bit embarrassing, but she liked to be sure to have a snack on hand at all times. "I only put snacks in there. I wrap everything in napkins. They're fine to eat, no different than a doggy bag."

"Of course they are, dear." Elspeth picked her sandwich up and took a big bite. "Delicious."

"Do you really think Celia was having an affair?" Ida asked, forking up a blob of egg salad that had fallen out of the sandwich and onto her plate. "A younger woman marrying an older man can be suspicious sometimes. Especially a *rich* older man."

"It's possible." Elspeth pinched a corner off her sandwich and chewed thoughtfully. "Money and passion are always good motives for murder."

A movement at the corner of the garden caught Ida's eye. It was one of those cats she'd seen on Elspeth's patio, and now it was sitting atop the wall looking like it was going to jump down onto *her* patio. She picked up a napkin and waved it in the cat's direction. "Shoo. Go away!"

Elspeth shot her a shocked look. "You don't like cats?"

"No. They're furtive and sneaky."

"They are not. They are wise and loving."

Ida eyed the cat with suspicion. She'd never really had much experience with cats, but they didn't seem to behave or do things on command, which in her eyes, made them quite useless. Maybe Elspeth knew more than she did, though. "I noticed they hang around your patio a lot."

"I seem to have a way with them. I have quite a few of them back home and volunteer to take care of the feral cats in town." Elspeth smiled fondly at the cat that was still atop the wall looking warily at Ida. "You should try to get to know them."

"I don't know." Ida looked at the cat who blinked at her with a haughty superiority that she had to admit she sort of admired. "I'm only used to dogs. My friend's granddaughter has one named Sprinkles. She's adorable, but she minds her manners and sits when you tell her to."

"Does she help you solve crimes?"

"What?" Was the woman joking? "Of course not. She's a dog."

"I didn't think so. Cats can help with investigations. You should consider getting one. I assume you like to investigate murders back home."

"Help? How?" Ida wondered if Elspeth was crazy as she assessed the cat with new interest.

"They are very intelligent. They seem to know things and can get into places humans can't. And if you watch them carefully, they will show you things," Elspeth said.

Ida scowled at the cat and turned her attention to her sandwich. She'd be the laughingstock of the Ladies' Detective Club if she suggested they get a cat to help them. Did they even allow cats in the retirement village? She reluctantly found herself thinking it might be nice to have a furry companion in her apartment.

"You'll see," Elspeth said quietly as she took the program for the flower show out of her purse. "The orchid contest is scheduled for two p.m. I say we go to the competition tent well before that. The contestants should be in their places primping their plants, and we can see if Celia really is going to show John's orchids. And if she is, we can try to question her."

"Good idea. I want to check out Kenneth Fairlane's tools. If he's missing a spade, it might be a reason to look into him further." Ida took a sip of lemonade. "He seems very serious about his orchids. Maybe he saw killing John as his only way to win first prize."

Elspeth nodded. "We mustn't rule anyone out. Money and passion are good motives, but a long, festering rivalry is one too."

"I wouldn't mind talking to Derek Keswick either. Maybe we can find Violet Crosby and get her to introduce us. We could pretend we are interested in healing vibes for flowers or whatever it is the man does." Ida patted her lips with a napkin and started putting the dishes on the tray.

"A fine idea. It shouldn't be too hard to find Violet.

She seems to be everywhere." Elspeth put her plate and glass on the tray then waved Ida off. "I'll do the dishes."

"Violet *does* seem to be everywhere, doesn't she?"

Elspeth stopped and looked back at Ida. "That is a bit suspicious, now that you mention it. And what was all that whispering to Judith in the butterfly tent? I know she was talking about Edith with the development plans—another reason to be suspicious of Edith, I might add. But what motive would Violet have?"

Ida shrugged. "She's a member of the Village Protection Committee and would not have liked the idea of Crowley Hall turning into a golf course."

"Indeed." Elspeth started toward the house. "As I said, we can't discount anyone. We'll pay close attention to Violet too."

Ida pushed up from the table, taking with her the iPad she'd brought outside. At first, she'd planned to FaceTime with Mona, Ruth, and Helen to go over the clues, but now that she had Elspeth here to toss around ideas with, she didn't see the point. Besides, it would be a lot more fun to solve the case on her own, with Elspeth's help, and then tell the ladies about it when she got home.

Though Ida loved working with the other ladies, Mona always seemed to think that *she* was the one who solved the cases, and Ida had to admit it would feel good to prove that she was just as good at putting together the clues as Mona was.

As she followed Elspeth into the cottage, she cast one backwards look at the wall. The cat was still there staring straight at her. She sensed a challenge in its gaze. Maybe there really was more to the furry felines than she had previously given them credit for.

CHAPTER 9

The competition tent was curiously empty, considering the judging would happen in an hour. Maybe the contestants were all resting. As such, it wasn't too hard to spot Derek Keswick. He was standing at a table, hands hovering a few inches above a brilliant-blue potted orchid.

As they approached, the ladies heard him chanting a mantra.

"Ohmmmm. Ohmmmm. Ohmmmm."

Ida coughed, and Derek's eyes flew open, his hands dropping to his sides.

"Sorry, didn't mean to disturb you." Ida sounded sincere, but Elspeth knew she actually had meant to disturb him.

Derek frowned. "Can I help you?"

"We were just coming to look at the orchids. We heard there was a contest, and some very rare species are to be exhibited." Elspeth looked around the tent and did her best to appear confused. "But I thought this was Sir John's table. I heard he always wins."

"It is his table." Derek looked suspicious of them.

"Well, then what are *you* doing here?" Ida asked. Elspeth was learning that the other woman could be a bit blunt. She always did it in the most charming way, though, kind of like a manipulative Betty White.

"I'm giving the plants spiritual fertilizer." Derek hovered his hands over the top of the flower again and closed his eyes, apparently dismissing them.

Ida wouldn't be so easily dismissed, though. "So this *is* Sir John's table. We were afraid his flowers wouldn't be shown, considering the... you know... accident."

Derek's eyes flew open again, his hands still hovering. "His widow is showing the orchids. This win was very important to Sir John, and she wanted to carry on."

"That's lovely," Ida said.

Elspeth noticed Ida kept glancing at the table next to them. Was that Kenneth Fairlane's table? There were only two other competitors in the tent, and both were women, so Fairlane wasn't here. She'd like to get a look at his tools. Perhaps after they were done inter-rogating Derek.

"Were you close to Sir John?" Elspeth asked.

Derek raised his hands above the plant again. "Not really."

"The wife, then? Celia?" Ida pushed. "I did hear you were good friends."

The way she accentuated the word "friends" and leaned in toward Derek had him frowning again.

"I don't know if you would say that." He waved his hands over the plant.

"Maybe John didn't like that you were friends," Ida persisted.

Derek's lips quirked in a lopsided smile that made him look handsome. Elspeth wondered why he was smiling, given Ida's accusatory tone. "If you're trying to insinuate that I have an inappropriate relationship with my client, I can assure you that's not the case."

"Client?" Elspeth and Ida said at the same time then glanced at each other.

"Indeed. I do spiritual work on both plants and humans." Derek closed his eyes again. "Now, if you ladies will excuse me."

"So you were treating Celia Hastings?" Ida asked.

Derek gave an exasperated sigh and let his hands

drop loudly to his sides. "That's what I just said, didn't I?"

"For what?" Elspeth asked.

"Sorry, I don't give out that sort of information about my clients." Derek was no longer smiling, and Elspeth got the impression they'd worn out their welcome.

"Interesting. But you were here early this morning before the show started, weren't you?"

Derek's eyes narrowed. "Yeah, so?"

"Well, I was just wondering if maybe you saw something," Ida said.

Relief flitted across Derek's face. "Oh, I thought you might be insinuating I had something to do with Sir John's death."

"Lordy, no!" Ida acted horrified, then her gaze turned shrewd. "Why would you think that?"

"No reason." Derek glanced around the tent.

"So what were you doing here this morning?" Elspeth asked.

"Mrs. Crosby asked me to come in and work on her prized petunias. It seems some of them were a bit droopy. I met her at the gate, and she got me the early-entry stamp." Derek showed them the stamp on the back of his hand, which was blue, not red like Elspeth's and Ida's. "Then she showed me which ones to work on. Did a bang-up job, too, if I do say so myself. Those flowers perked right up."

Elspeth studied the young man. He appeared to be telling the truth, though she sensed there was a secret that had to do with Celia Hastings. But even if they were having an affair, that didn't necessarily make him a killer. She made a mental note to double-check with Mrs. Crosby whether or not his story and timing were true.

"And what time was that?" Ida asked.

Derek shrugged. "About an hour before the start."

Ida glanced at Elspeth. Though they didn't know the exact time the murder had occurred, it was likely an hour before the show started, given what they did know.

"Did you see anything unusual?" Elspeth tried to put a kindly tone in her voice. Since Ida was being a bit brusque, she figured to play good cop to Ida's bad cop.

"Not really. I was hardly the only one here, though." Derek made a show of flexing his fingers and then held his hands above the flower again. Elspeth sensed his patience with them was running low, and their interrogation was just about over.

"Who else was here?" Ida asked.

Derek sighed again. "Well, there are always plenty

of people here to set up before the opening. I don't know all of them, but if you want to know who was in the back near the koi pond, you should ask Edith Wilson."

Elspeth heard Ida's sharp intake of breath at the name of the one person on the Village Protection Committee they had yet to talk to.

"She was here early this morning?" Elspeth asked.

"Not exactly here. She was in the woods at the edge of the show. There are no fences around to keep people from sneaking in that way, even though there is clearly an entry gate where one should pay a fee." Derek pursed his lips, indicating his disapproval of people sneaking in without paying the fee. Elspeth agreed.

"She was sneaking in?" Ida asked.

Derek shrugged. "What else would she be doing out there? The whole village knows that they can easily get in from the path in the woods. It goes right past the koi pond, and even though Adelaide put up topiaries with velvet ropes strung between them to indicate where the show technically ends, plenty of villagers just step over the ropes to sneak in. Even Kenneth isn't above sneaking into the show." Derek thrust his chin out, and Elspeth turned to see a man with a wheelbarrow backing through the flap at the back of the tent.

The man, presumably Kenneth Fairlane, turned around, his face darkening when he saw them. He wheeled over to the table next to them, his eyes on Derek.

"I see you've brought something from your greenhouse. Secret orchid strain?" Derek craned his neck to see into the wheelbarrow.

Kenneth stepped protectively in front of the wheelbarrow and gave the orchid Derek was working on a pointed look. "At least I don't have to resort to mumbo jumbo to get mine to grow."

Derek raised one brow. "Ha! You know my methods work. At least I don't cover up the panes of my greenhouse so I can work in secret."

"There are spies everywhere. I need to keep my methods a secret." Kenneth turned and started to unload the wheelbarrow. Elspeth and Ida both craned to look inside as he took out a small bag of bark mix and placed it on the table before reaching in to pull out a snow-white and pale-yellow orchid. Cradling the pot like a newborn baby, he placed it gently on the table, leaving only a brand-new set of potting tools in the wheelbarrow. There was no spade.

"Is that why you snuck into the show the back way?" Ida asked.

"What? I didn't sneak into the show." Kenneth was indignant. "I pay my way the same as anyone."

"Not true!" Derek yelled. "I saw you lurking over by the hedge maze, near the path in the woods."

"I wasn't lurking." Kenneth's pale cheeks were tinged with red. "I was going for a walk in the woods."

"Yeah, sure. I don't have time for this. The judging is in an hour, and I still need to imbue some vibes into Gertrude here." Derek gestured at the orchid then gave Ida and Elspeth a pointed look. "So if you people would leave me alone…"

Ida nodded at Elspeth, and they sidled over in front of Kenneth's table while Derek went back to chanting at the orchid.

"Looks like your biggest competitor is still in the running," Ida said.

Kenneth narrowed his gaze at her. "Weren't you in here before asking about orchids?"

"I'm a big orchid fan."

Kenneth looked at Ida over the tops of his wire-rimmed glasses, his face darkening. "Fan or competitor? Are you here on a spying mission?" He slid the orchid away from Ida as if he thought she might snatch it off the table. "You're not in the contest, are you?"

"Of course not." Ida said. "I'm visiting. I'm just a spectator."

Kenneth looked as if he didn't believe her as he slid the orchid even further away. Then he turned to the cabinet behind him. "Doesn't matter. I'm not worried about you or anyone else. I know I have the winning plant." He shot a glance in Derek's direction as he dug a key out of his pocket and placed it in the lock to the cabinet.

Elspeth held her breath as he opened the cabinet. She and Ida craned their necks so they could look over his shoulder to see what was inside.

Ida gasped. Sitting right there in the front of the cabinet was a brand-new spade.

IDA'S PACE was brisk as they left the competition tent. The case was coming together. She felt it in her bones.

"Just because Kenneth has a new spade doesn't mean that his old one is broken," Elspeth said as if reading her mind.

"Doesn't mean it's not. At any rate, it bears looking into."

"I agree. But what about Derek? Do you think he was lying?" Elspeth asked.

Ida slowed her pace. Derek hadn't acted like he was lying. Then again, he was sort of an odd duck. "Taking care of Sir John's orchids is a funny thing for his killer to do, but I suppose it might be just the way to cast suspicion away from him."

"Do you really think that Celia and Derek would go to those lengths? I mean, it's not really necessary for her to carry on with the orchids. No one expects that of her." Elspeth shook her head and continued. "It's a little over-the-top and only draws attention to them. Wouldn't be the smartest move if one or both of them were the killer."

"Maybe Celia is just a client," Ida said. "But he was acting evasive about that, and Judith implied Celia was hanging around to see Derek as if something more was going on between them."

"Could be that Celia didn't want anyone knowing she was seeing him. Maybe she was embarrassed about it or was being treated for some ailment she didn't want anyone to know about."

They turned down a path that led past a crop of gigantic sunflowers. Ida marveled at how tall they were, standing above her by a good foot—not that that said much since she was only a few inches over five feet tall herself. Still, they were a bit scary-looking with their giant flowers the sizes of dinner plates.

"Could be," Ida said, backing away from one particular sunflower that seemed to be looming over her as if it would bow down and smother her. "It bears further investigation, but so does Kenneth Fairlane."

"Yes, Kenneth is a much more likely suspect, I think." Elspeth stopped to inspect the center of one of the shorter flowers. This one was more their height, and Ida noticed the dozens of black seeds in its center. "We need to get a look at his greenhouse."

Ida turned to her. "Do you think he would be stupid enough to keep the top broken part of the spade in there? I would think the killer would have dispensed with that by now."

"But where? The police are looking at all the usual places. One can't simply toss it away." Elspeth continued down the path. "Besides, there is something fishy about that greenhouse. Derek mentioned he kept some of the glass covered. No one does that. The whole point of a greenhouse is to have the sun shine in."

"Indeed. If only we could figure out how to get in. I don't think Kenneth trusts me now and—"

"Save the village! Sign the change of use petition!"

Ida was interrupted by someone yelling nearby, the voice disturbingly familiar.

Ida clutched Elspeth's arm. "Did you hear what I just heard?"

"I certainly did. That's the voice from the path! That could be the killer!"

heir view was blocked on all sides by tall trees and flower displays, but Elspeth had a keen sense of direction and homed in on the location of the voice. Luckily, the woman kept bellowing, giving Elspeth a constant sound to follow. When she got to an intersecting path, an orange-striped cat trotted down the west side, and they turned down that path to see a short, pudgy, middle-aged woman standing near an abundance of trellises. She was waving a clipboard in the air.

"Please, sign the petition." She shoved the clipboard in front of a couple walking with a red-headed toddler between them, and they sidestepped so as to avoid her.

Elspeth admired the display of trellis flowers as they proceeded toward the woman. It was like a maze of vines with wisteria, nasturtium, and trumpet vines growing on all types of trellises. There were benches with large trellises behind them, round arbors with morning glories climbing, and tall fan-like trellises with purple leatherflowers. It was like a secret garden with a maze of vines growing everywhere.

The woman spotted them heading her way. She smiled, her expression reminding Elspeth of a praying mantis that had just spotted willing prey.

"What's this about saving the village?" Elspeth asked, playing dumb in the hopes that the woman would say something suspicious. Elspeth didn't know for sure, but odds were that the woman was the one person they had yet to talk to—Edith Wilson. They'd met everyone else from the Village Protection Committee, and who else would be running around with a petition?

"The whole village is at risk." The woman spread her arms to indicate the area. "They want to make it into a golf course!"

"Surely not the *whole* village," Ida said.

The woman's gaze narrowed at them. "Well, most of it. Are you from around here? You look familiar, but your accent is foreign."

"I'm Elspeth Whipple, and this is my friend Ida Johnston." Elspeth gestured toward Ida, pleased that the woman had given her the perfect opportunity to find out who she was. "Are you a member of the Village Protection Committee?"

"Yes, yes. I'm Edith Wilson. How do you know of the committee?"

Elspeth nodded. "Oh, I've talked to a few members in the tea tent and such. Great work your committee does. Now, tell us about this petition."

"Oh, it's just awful what they plan to do. They'll turn Crowley Hall into a hotel and golf course! The village will be ruined, and the Twigsledge Flower Show will become a thing of the past."

"Oh dear." Ida tsked and shook her head. "But surely they can't just do that, can they? I mean, there must be rules about that sort of thing over here."

"Yes, they apply for a change of use. But you see, it's set to allow for a hotel." Edith held the clipboard out. "That's why I started the petition. We need to vote to rezone, then they won't be able to construct this horrid atrocity."

Elspeth leaned over to look at the petition. Zero signatures. "Well now, didn't I hear something about the owner of Crowley Hall being the one who died this morning? I would think that would change the situation, wouldn't it?"

Edith's gaze narrowed. She didn't look too upset

about the mention of the death, but did she look guilty? "I couldn't say for sure. Depends on the will and the terms of sale, I suppose."

Elspeth was skeptical. Did she really not know if the death would make a difference? If she did, then why would she be collecting signatures? Maybe she wasn't a hundred percent sure, and this was an insurance policy in case killing Sir John didn't change things. Or maybe it was her way of covering up the fact that she was the killer.

"Such a tragic death," Elspeth said. "Did you know the victim? You must have, seeing as you are so involved with the village."

Edith's expression held a note of suspicion as her gaze darted between Ida and Elspeth. "I knew him. Didn't think he should sell the hall, though."

"Well, then I'm very sorry for your loss," Elspeth said. "You were here at the show early this morning, weren't you?"

"What?" Edith uttered. "No! I was not here early."

"Oh, that's funny. I thought I saw you. I was one of the first to arrive, but maybe I was mistaken." It was a little lie, but Elspeth *had* been one of the first to arrive, and Adelaide had said she'd seen Edith, which must have been just as the show was about to start—after Sir John was killed. But now Elspeth wondered where, exactly, she had seen her. Was it inside the show or skulking around in the woods as Derek had claimed? "And I believe Adelaide Timmons mentioned seeing you."

Edith's eyes darted around as if she were trying to find the best escape route. She took a small step backward on the path that led deeper into the maze of trellises. "I didn't arrive early this morning. I had important business. It wasn't early when I saw Adelaide over at the daisies, so I don't know what she's getting at."

"The daisies?" Ida asked.

"Out in the common. She picks them for those tall vases at the gate," Edith said.

"Was that before or after you went walking around in the woods?" Ida asked.

"Walking around in the woods?" She took another step away. "What do you mean?"

Ida took a step closer to Edith. "I'm pretty sure that Derek—you know, that guy who does all the hoodoo hippie stuff to the plants." Ida mimed holding her palms over the plants and *ohm*-ed. "He said that he saw you lurking around in the woods near the koi pond where people try to sneak in."

"I was not trying to *sneak* in," Edith said indignantly. "I was simply going for my walk, and I... wait a minute. Who are you people, and why were you talking to Derek about me?"

"We're naturally inquisitive," Ida said. "Have you got something to hide?"

Edith frowned. "No."

"Well, then you won't mind telling us what you were talking about early this morning when you were walking the path on Primrose Lane behind the cottages. You know, the ones with all the flower names."

"What are you talking about?" Edith looked genuinely perplexed.

Ida fisted her hands on her hips. "Don't play dumb. We heard you. You practically confessed to the murder."

Edith gasped. "I never! Have you been following me? Who put you up to this?"

"Now, now, no one has been following you." Elspeth used her most soothing tone. She was finding out that Ida could get a little hot-headed, and she didn't want to scare Edith off. They hadn't gotten all the information they needed out of her yet.

"Yeah, we overheard you from our patios," Ida said. "And you said you'd fixed things, and the village would change over your dead body. That seems mighty suspicious given the circumstances."

"Well, it's not. I don't appreciate these accusations, and I said over *my* dead body, not over John's. Besides, I wasn't anywhere near the koi pond when he was killed. I was in the... um..."

Two figures stepped out from behind a tall trellis loaded with the most gorgeous hot-pink bougainvillea Elspeth had ever seen. The plant was a perfectly lush specimen packed with flowers. No wonder Elspeth hadn't seen Louise James and Max Evans lurking behind it.

"You were at the what?" Louise asked Edith.

Edith's eyes grew bigger, and she sputtered. "At the woods. I was taking my walk."

"Do you always walk in the woods?"

"Yes, I go there rather often." Edith raised her chin as if challenging the detective to prove her wrong.

Louise looked at Elspeth and Ida. "And what are you two doing here? Seems like you show up everywhere."

Elspeth couldn't be sure, but she thought the detective might be trying to repress a smile. Elspeth, on the other hand, was not smiling. She wasn't happy that the detective had barged in on their interrogation when they were just about to crack the case. Judging by the scowl on Ida's face, she felt the same.

"We're just enjoying the flower show. Ida's favorite

flower is the morning glory, isn't it, Ida?" Elspeth said, jabbing Ida in the ribs at her confused look.

"Oh, yes. Yes, it is. I particularly like this one." Ida started over toward a trellis with a jewel-red nasturtium on it, and Elspeth took her elbow, rerouting her to a lovely purple morning glory threaded around a scrolly wrought-iron triangular-shaped structure.

Louise's left brow curved up. "Uh huh."

Edith was trying to inch away, and Louise turned back to her. "So, tell me about this walk. Do you always trespass on the Crowley Hall estate?"

"I… well… I wasn't exactly trespassing. I mean, the grounds have been open to the village for centuries. We always walk there."

Elspeth and Ida pretended to admire the morning glory while listening to the conversation. Elspeth glanced back and saw Louise cross her arms over her chest. The expression on her face was impassive, but her body language told Elspeth she didn't believe a word Edith was saying.

Should she tell the detectives what they'd overheard on the path behind their cottages? Or that Judith had told Violet she saw Edith getting the development plan for the grounds? Elspeth was almost positive now that Edith was the killer. But maybe they wouldn't tell Louise—she was a bit intimidating despite her frumpy initial appearance. That nice Max might be better to talk to.

"You do?" Louise asked Edith. "Then why were you at the town hall early this morning getting a map of the property? If you always walk there, then surely you would know where to walk."

Darn! They already knew about the map. But they didn't know about the conversation Elspeth had overheard. She edged closer to Max.

"I do. I mean, I know most of the paths, but the plan shows all of them and I—"

"And you had the town offices open early for this purpose, perhaps to hide what you were doing?" Louise leaned closer to Edith. Elspeth recognized her technique. She'd cut Edith off on purpose and was leaning into her in order to get Edith flustered. It was working.

"No! Not really. Shirley just opens whenever we have a need." Edith straightened. "That's how it works in small villages."

Elspeth inspected a gorgeous, soft-pink clematis that was climbing up a tall trellis, which just happened to be very close to Louise and Edith.

"It still seems a bit odd to me that you wouldn't know all the paths already. I mean, you've lived here most of your life and walk there every day," Louise said.

"I... well..." Edith sputtered.

"Maybe what you really wanted was the exact route to make your getaway," Max, who had been standing there quietly, said.

"Getaway from what?" Edith said.

"From murdering Sir John." Louise's tone was cold.

"I didn't murder him!"

"The evidence is against you." Max took out handcuffs. "It's no secret you were bitterly opposed to him selling the hall."

"And there is some question as to whether that will go through now since all the paperwork hasn't been signed," Louise said.

Elspeth admired their technique. They were standing on either side of Edith, peppering her with questions so she had to swivel her head back and forth between them, thus throwing her off balance and adding to her presumably already heightened state of anxiety. It was a great technique to speed up a confession, though she and Ida could have gotten one just as easily.

"Sir John was bashed in the head and pushed into the koi pond about an hour before the show started."

Max stepped closer to Edith, pulled out a notepad, and consulted it. "But we've talked to everyone who worked the show, from Adelaide Timmons on down to Charlie at the front gate, and no one who wasn't supposed to be inside the gates before the show started was seen. So that means the killer escaped through the woods."

Beads of sweat formed atop Edith's lips, and she wrung her hands. Louise stepped in closer, and now she and Max were practically on top of the poor woman. "Give it up, Mrs. Wilson. Tell the truth. The development plan shows all the paths on the property and wanted that so you could plan your escape through the woods after you killed Sir John!"

"No! I tell you, I didn't kill him!"

Max's handcuffs glinted in the sun. "Then why were you seen in the woods at the time of the murder?"

Edith collapsed onto a bench. "Fine! I'll tell you. I *was* in the woods."

"Aha!" Ida's shout earned a stern look from Louise. Ida's expression turned sheepish, and she immediately pretended to be inspecting an orange trumpet vine. "I thought these things had yellow stamens, and turns out I was right. Oh, did I interrupt? Sorry, I wasn't listening in or anything."

Edith sobbed, and Louise turned her attention back to her.

"Why were you sneaking around in the woods?" Louise asked her again.

"I was sneaking around but not because I was running away from killing John. I was doing something else in there." Edith said the last part softly, looking down at her hands.

"What, exactly, was that?" Max asked.

Edith sighed. "I was moving the landmarks and stakes of the boundary lines so that when the golf course surveyor came out, he would determine the site wasn't suitable."

Louise's brows ticked up. "You expect us to believe that?"

Edith looked panicked. "I can show you where I moved the metal pins from. There's protected swamp land out there demarcated by granite markers and metal pins. I thought if I moved them to make it look like the golf course would run through the swamp land, the deal would fall through. That's why I got the development plan, so I could see the proposed boundaries for the golf course."

Louise and Max exchanged a look.

"Can anyone corroborate this?" Louise asked.

"Well, I told Jared Pennysworth this morning."

Edith shot a glare at Elspeth. So that must have been what she meant when she said she'd "fixed things."

"Did anyone see you doing this?" Max asked.

"I don't think so. But someone else might have had the same idea, because someone had been digging out there." Edith pressed her lips together. "Though it wasn't near the stakes. Anyway, the only other person I saw out in the woods was Kenneth Fairlane, but he didn't see me. He was too busy trying to navigate with his full wheelbarrow."

"Derek saw you near the koi pond, but he didn't say what time," Max said.

Elspeth glanced at him. Had they also talked to Derek, or had they been listening in on her and Ida's conversation with him?

"What about going in or coming out of the woods?" Louise asked. "That might help us with timing."

"There was someone!" Edith sounded hopeful. "When I was coming out of the path afterwards, I saw Adelaide Timmons. She was picking flowers for the show, so that might help determine the timing, as she always picks those before the show so they can have vases full at the gates when it opens. Maybe she'll know exactly when she picked them, and that can help determine my whereabouts at the time of the um... murder."

"We'll be sure to talk to her. And Kenneth too." Louise glanced at Max, who put his handcuffs away.

"Am I free to go?" Edith looked surprised.

"For now," Louise said. "But don't go far. We'll want to see these markers you dug up and the development plan after we talk to Adelaide and Kenneth."

Edith shot up from the bench. "Of course, no problem. Talk to you later." She scurried off into the maze of trellises.

Elspeth was disappointed that Edith hadn't confessed, but she was inclined to believe the woman's story. She had sounded sincere enough, and she doubted the woman could make up something so elaborate on the fly. Still, she'd like to see for herself those pins that had been moved. Oh well, some things had to be left to the police. She'd just have to trust that they would verify that.

She and Ida moved on to a display of hollyhocks. She didn't want to be too obvious by rushing off right away, but as soon as the police left, she'd suggest they go find Kenneth Fairlane's greenhouse.

"Not so fast, ladies." Louise had come to stand next to them, her expression flat.

"Whatever do you mean?" Ida asked. "Surely you don't want to question us. We didn't see what Edith was doing this morning."

"I see what *you* two are doing. I heard you interrogating Edith. I'll have to warn you to stop. It could be dangerous to confront suspects." Louise actually did look concerned. "Someone here is a killer."

"Oh, we wouldn't do anything dangerous." Ida turned to Elspeth. "Would we, dear?"

Elspeth shook her head. "Certainly not."

"That's good to know, because if I find you interrogating dangerous suspects, I might have to keep you safe by throwing you in jail."

"Well, we wouldn't want that," Elspeth said.

"Nope, we'll be as good as a spring rain," Ida added.

"We're just headed off for some afternoon tea now." Elspeth took Ida's arm, and they started down the path, the weight of Louise's stare burning a hole in their backs.

CHAPTER 11

"*D*o you think they'll stop investigating?" Max asked as they watched Ida and Elspeth walk away.

"I doubt it, but hopefully we can get ahead of them so that they don't endanger themselves." Louise could tell by their purposeful strides and the way they were obviously trying not to look back at her that they weren't going to let this go. She half regretted using them to get information, but the truth was that she wouldn't have been able to get the villagers to open up. Of course, she would never put a citizen in danger. She knew the killer wouldn't resort to inflicting violence on them just because they were asking uncomfortable questions. This killer had a specific purpose and wouldn't rush adding to their body count unless it was someone who could implicate them in the murder.

"At least Edith confirmed our suspicions," Max said.

Louise turned to look down the path that Edith Wilson had exited. "Yeah, now we have a witness who saw Kenneth Fairlane in the woods, and we can go ahead with the search warrant of his greenhouse."

"Do you really think he has the murder weapon hidden in there?" Max asked.

"He's been acting very suspicious and had two reasons to want John Hastings dead. Besides, no one covers up greenhouse glass unless they have something to hide." Louise leaned over to smell a pretty orange, tube-like flower. She had no idea of the names of these things, but at least the displays were easy to hide behind. A fat bee buzzed near her nose, and she pulled back.

Max pulled out his phone and started typing. Checking on the status of the search warrant, Louise hoped. The sooner they could get to Kenneth Hastings's place and check it out the better. She hoped Elspeth and Ida weren't onto him too.

"Nothing on the warrant yet." Max put his phone away, and they started walking toward the exit. "So, you buy her story about moving the stakes?"

"We'll check it out, but I think she was telling the truth. According to the town clerk, the plan did show the paths along with the boundaries and the plans for the new golf course." Louise sidestepped some kind of flowering shrub whose branches had reached out into the path.

"Weird that the town offices just open up at random times," Max said.

"Yeah, but lucky thing Angie Hastings saw her there." Louise said. They'd interviewed Angie Hastings before running into Edith. Angie and her aunt Judith Hastings had been at the town offices themselves at a very odd hour that morning. They'd been looking into the legalities of the Crowley Hall sale. The timing was such that it provided them an alibi for the time of the murder, so Louise had reluctantly crossed them off her list. They each had a good motive but couldn't have done it. Their alibis had been verified by Shirley.

"EVEN WEIRDER that so many people were there," Max added. Max shrugged. "Village life certainly is confusing with all the hidden relationships and nefarious goings-on. Give me the city life any day. These small villages are full of secrets and lies."

"Tell me about it." Louise saw the exit at the end of

the path and picked up the pace. She didn't like being assigned to these village investigations. The people were so closemouthed, and it always seemed that everyone was covering something up. Much as she'd prefer a more straightforward serial killer case or a city murder, she'd drawn the short straw and been assigned this case and was determined to do her best.

IDA NUDGED Elspeth down a path to the right and, after a few steps, glanced back to see if the detectives were following them. To her relief, the path behind them was empty.

"How do you like that? Those detectives were listening in on our interrogations!"

"It's unconscionable!" Elspeth scowled. "Can you believe she swooped right in just as we were about to get Edith to confess?"

"Yeah, except I don't think that Edith is the killer." Ida glanced at Elspeth to see if she agreed with her assessment, which judging by the look on her face, she did.

"I know, but *we* could have discovered that just as well as the police."

"Yes, but it worked in our favor, I suppose, because

we got that little tidbit about no one being seen at the show early this morning who wasn't supposed to be here."

"Right. That means the killer escaped through the woods."

"And Edith herself said she saw Kenneth with his wheelbarrow full." Elspeth turned down a path with a sign toward the exit.

"That, combined with the fact that he had a brand-new spade in his tool cabinet, warrants further investigation." Ida picked up the pace.

"You bet it does." Elspeth trotted along beside her. "It might help if we knew where he lives."

"We could ask someone, but who? Maybe Violet Crosby. She seems to know everything. We'd probably find her in the tea tent."

Elspeth scanned the crowd. "I see Adelaide Timmons way over there. We could ask her, but she seems busy with hauling large branches somewhere."

Ida followed her gaze to see a tall woman in yellow boots, gesturing wildly at some poor high school student. She didn't want to go all the way back and interrupt her. "We're almost at the exit. Going back now would slow us down."

"Good point. We know he lives next door to Crowley Hall, so his place shouldn't be too hard to find." Elspeth stopped short as a black-and-white tuxedo cat darted out in front of them then ran out the exit and veered to the left. "And I think I know exactly which direction we should go."

Ida didn't want to be rude to her new friend, but she highly doubted a cat was going to show them the way to Kenneth Fairlane's greenhouse. She humored Elspeth, though, since they needed to walk around in order to find it anyway.

The cat trotted ahead of them, his tail held high, as they walked past the edge of the flower show where a flower-laden white-picket fence lined the street. The cat turned onto the brick walkway, under the rose-covered arbor, and around the side of a rather large cottage with an arched oak door.

"Look! It's right back here!" Elspeth practically ran around the side of the house. "I told you that cats were useful."

Ida didn't reply. They knew Kenneth lived next to Crowley Hall, so the cat did have a fifty-fifty chance of picking the right direction.

The backyard of the house was loaded with flowers. Lovely flower beds were set up in a formal style with a birdbath in the middle. At the edge of the property backing up to the woods was a glass greenhouse. One section of it had paper taped up to the glass. The forest was the same one that was next to Crowley Hall, and it would be an easy shortcut for Kenneth to take his wheelbarrow through the woods to get back and forth from the flower show.

The greenhouse was loaded with plants, making it difficult to see inside, but looking between the leaves, Ida could see several tables with various tools and planter pots on top. At one of those tables, Kenneth Fairlane appeared to be coaxing a tall orchid into a decorative pot.

Elspeth stopped at the door. "Should we knock?"

"I suppose so." Ida didn't see another door, so it wasn't as if Kenneth could escape. They'd have him cornered in there and could call the police once they had the evidence.

Elspeth rapped on the door. Kenneth jerked his head up and looked in their direction.

"Yoo-hoo, Kenneth. We came to see your green-house!" Ida yelled in a sing-song voice as if Kenneth would welcome their visit.

He opened the door. His expression was not welcoming. "What are you two doing here?"

Ida craned to see over his shoulder, and he moved so he was in her way. Something to hide?

"We had such a lovely conversation at the flower

show, and you practically invited us over to see your wonderful greenhouse," Ida said.

"I did?"

"Yes, and we're so excited!" Elspeth managed to slip inside, and Kenneth moved away from the door. "Hey, watch out! My prize orchids are in here!"

Kenneth started toward Elspeth, probably to usher her out, but it gave Ida the chance to slip in as well. She looked around, focusing on trying to find the handle of a spade, but she didn't see any handles just lying about. A new set of tools leaned against a table, but that in itself wasn't really suspicious.

Now that Ida was inside, she could see that one section of the greenhouse had been blocked off and closed in with a solid wall and door. That was the section that had the glass panes covered in paper. But now she could see only the side panes were covered. The top panes still let the sun in. It looked like a great place to hide evidence, but why wouldn't Kenneth just throw the handle of the murder weapon away?

"Uh… this really isn't a good time." Kenneth rushed over to Elspeth, who had wandered down to the end of a table and was looking at a large ficus plant.

"Oh, we won't bother you for very long. We just wanted to see how you set things up here." Elspeth put her hand on a heavy iron garden hoe that looked brand new. "I see you have new tools. I find it's so much nicer to do gardening with new tools, don't you?"

Kenneth grabbed the rake away from her. "Yes. Well, I haven't had new tools for a while. I was due."

Ida watched him carefully. He seemed very nervous that she was asking about the tools.

"Are these the orchids for the contest?" Elspeth stood in front of six gorgeous plants all lined up in earthenware pots.

"Yes. Yes, they are. In fact, I better get them over to the tent. The judging is in an hour." Kenneth rolled the wheelbarrow over and started loading it. "If you ladies will excuse me…"

Ida caught Elspeth's eye and inclined her head toward the blocked-off section as she inched toward it.

"Of course. I'd wish you luck, but I guess you don't need it with these beauties. Now, I bet you have a ringer up your sleeve. Perhaps in this room?"

Kenneth jerked his head in her direction, alarm flickering across his expression as he saw Ida standing there with her hand on the knob. "No! Don't go in there."

"Oh, why not?" Elspeth had come to join Ida. "We won't tell your secret."

"Yeah, you can trust us. Just one little peek." Ida turned the knob, surprised that it wasn't locked.

"No, don't! You can't go in there!" Kenneth's voice had turned menacing, but that didn't stop Ida from pushing the door open. The section was small. Shaded light filtered in from the covered glass panes on the sides and full sun from the top. What was in there was not what she'd expected at all.

"I told you not to go in there." The tone in Kenneth's voice startled Ida. It was tinged with dread and resolve. She turned to see him standing only a foot away, holding a brand-new spade in his hand and looking as if he wanted to use it on them.

CHAPTER 12

*M*ax leaned against the doorway of Louise's office, where she was sitting at the desk with manila folders strewn about and papers hanging out. She was reading John Hastings's will. "We've searched every dumpster and backyard refuse pile in the village, and there's no sign of the handle of the murder weapon."

Louise sighed and sat back in the chair. "The killer must still have it. Who knows where, though?"

"Maybe they buried it. There's been a ton of digging and planting with this flower show. It could be under one of the displays," Max said.

"Or buried in the woods." Louise frowned. "Didn't Edith Wilson say that someone else had been digging there?"

Max nodded. "When she takes us out to the spots where she moved the stakes today, maybe we can take a look. Hopefully dig something up. Get it?"

Louise cracked a half-hearted smile at his joke. It seemed crass to joke about murder, but in their business one had to do something, or it got downright depressing. "The killer wouldn't want to get caught with it."

"Nope. And we're running out of suspects. Family members have alibis." Max cocked his head to look at the will she had on the desk in front of her. "Did you find anything in there?"

"No, it all goes to the wife, so only she would have a reason to kill him," Louise said. "And she can either continue with the sale of the hall or not. The papers weren't finalized, so now she can back out."

"But she didn't do it," Max said.

"Couldn't have... she was with the parish priest that morning." Louise had crossed Celia Hastings off her list an hour ago after verifying her alibi. If you couldn't trust the parish priest, who could you trust?

"Yeah, but she was very secretive about that. And Mrs. Crosby did tell us that Celia had said things would change for the family. I'd say Sir John dying was a big change," Max said.

Louise tapped the pen on the desk. "She could have had an accomplice."

"You mean Derek Keswick?"

"Rumor has it…"

Max laughed. "Well, Mrs. Crosby is the one who told us that, and you know how those village busy-bodies are. Always sensationalizing things. Besides, I don't think those affair rumors are true. Derek prefers men."

Louise frowned. Usually her instincts about that were spot-on. "Are you sure?"

"Absolutely."

"All righty then, I guess we go back to our prior motive. The killer didn't want the Crowley Hall sale to go through."

"But the sale could still go through if Celia wants it to."

"Maybe the killer didn't know that she would be in control of the sale?"

"Or maybe the killer did and is in cahoots with Celia and has persuaded her not to sell somehow."

"But why would Celia do that? She already has enough money and nothing to gain." Louise's blood chilled as she realized something. "What if the killer was working under the assumption that the sale would be halted, and now they find out that Celia can sell it just as easily?"

Max frowned. "Celia could be in trouble. Who would get the house after her?"

Louise glanced down at John's and Celia's wills. "If anything happens to Celia, and she still owns the property, it reverts to Angie."

"And Angie would give it to Judith."

"And Judith would never sell."

"But Judith and Angie have alibis," Max said.

"Right." Louise glanced at the fax machine. Where was that darn search warrant? "Those are verified by Shirley at the town hall, and she doesn't appear to have a stake in this so would have no reason to lie."

"There are quite a few others who wouldn't want the sale. Like this Village Protection Committee, for example."

"And Adelaide Timmons. That show is her whole life."

"And let's not forget Kenneth Fairlane. He lives next door, and his lifestyle would be severely disrupted by the new hotel."

"He seems like the jittery type, but he acted overly nervous when we talked to him and clearly wouldn't want the golf course."

"And he was seen in the woods."

"We need to get a look in that greenhouse, but we have to do it by the book, and we need that warrant. He could be dangerous. I just hope those mini Marples haven't come to the same conclusion. I hate to think what he would do to them if they confronted him. Or what he has hidden behind those covered-up pieces of glass."

As if on cue, the fax machine whirred to life, and Max picked up the paper it spit out. "The warrant just came through!"

"And not a moment too soon." Louise grabbed her keys. "Let's go before Kenneth does something drastic!"

"ORCHIDS?" Elspeth's tone dripped with disappointment as she looked around the room. It was very tidy, with one table that had about a dozen unusual-looking, small, creamy-white orchid plants in various stages of being potted. A bag of coconut husk chips and some peat moss sat in the corner. There were no tools, much less an incriminating broken handle from an old spade.

Kenneth sighed, and Elspeth turned to see him

lower the spade he'd been holding. "I meant to block the door with this." He hefted the spade.

"But why?" Ida asked. "What is so special about these orchids?"

Kenneth's expression turned sheepish, and the frail, thin man seemed to fold in on himself. "They're very rare. It's a secret."

Elspeth sensed there was more to it than the flowers being secret. But she knew that Kenneth needed a gentle touch in order to reveal what that was. Ida probably wasn't the person for that, so she smiled at Kenneth and used her softest tone. "They are very lovely. I could see why you would want to keep them secret. But why not enter them in the contest?"

"I can't. At least not now. You see, I didn't exactly get them through normal means." Kenneth's gaze moved over Elspeth's shoulder, and his face lit up as it rested on the orchids.

Ida shifted on her feet. Elspeth could tell she was getting restless. She'd better speed it up.

"Is that why you have the glass blocked off? So no one can see them?"

Kenneth nodded, his shoulders slumping even more.

Elspeth took him by the arm, removing the spade first just in case he really wanted to use it as a weapon like she'd thought when she'd seen him standing behind them. She led him to the cast-iron bench across from the orchids. Actually, it was rather pleasant with the sun only beaming in from the top and the sides papered up. "Why don't you tell us all about it?"

"I didn't mean to do anything dishonest, but they would be ruined if I didn't save them."

"Of course. I'm sure you did the right thing," Elspeth said to encourage a further confession. "How did you save them?"

"I was on one of my mid-day walks in the forest, and that's when I saw them." His gaze drifted to the orchids on the table, and his lips quirked up in a smile. "They're ghost orchids. A very rare variety, and to think that they were growing right in the forest!"

"So you dug them up?" Ida glanced at the spade.

"Yes, I even bought new tools because they were so precious. Didn't want to use old, rusty tools."

"What's so bad about that? Is there some law against picking flowers here? You folks do have some strange customs over here," Ida said.

"Not picking flowers, but digging them up from someone else's property is frowned upon." Kenneth's face turned sad. "But I had to do something! They would all be killed with that golf course. So I snuck out and grabbed a few a week. Been doing it for weeks now."

"But why hide them?" Elspeth asked. "Surely you would want to put them in the orchid show."

"Not right away. Too many questions would be asked. I need to learn how to propagate them first, so I can show that I grew the bulk of them."

"So that's why you were so secretive?" Elspeth asked.

Kenneth nodded. "The land belongs to Crowley Hall, and I didn't think Sir John would take kindly to stealing orchids from his land. But I also didn't think he cared about it. He was selling, after all."

"And that's why you killed him, right?" Ida asked.

"Killed him? I did no such thing. I was busy misting my orchids all morning right up until the time the show started. Contestants get early entry." Kenneth held his hand up to show the blue stamp. "I was here all morning. You can ask Violet Crosby, Jane Pennyfeather, George Dunfy, Adelaide Timmons, and Enid Brown. They all saw me at different times, as they were all in the tent early that morning."

A few of the names were familiar, but Elspeth doubted she and Ida would take the time to talk to them. The police could follow up on that. Besides, she had a good feeling that Kenneth was telling the truth.

Kenneth looked at Ida and then at Elspeth. "You ladies won't tell on me, will you?"

Elspeth didn't like telling on folks, but she had a feeling the police might want the same explanation as they did. "Well, I won't, but I think—"

"Police! Come out with your hands up, Kenneth!"

"Oh dear!" Kenneth's hands shook.

Poor guy. Elspeth felt sorry for him and wished she could give him a shot of courage. Maybe she could bake some special cookies or make a tea for him. She might be an old woman, but she was still able to work some magic when she wanted to, especially when it was laced in her food.

Ida raced to the door. "No need for that. I'm afraid you're a bit too late. We've already gotten a confession…"

DCI Louise James and Sergeant Max Evans appeared in the doorway, quizzical looks on their faces and nightsticks drawn. Once they saw the situation, they lowered their weapons.

"What is going on in here?" Louise asked.

Elspeth and Ida filled them in on Kenneth's confession and sat through a lecture by Louise.

"I *will* throw you in jail if you insist on pursuing this. The killer is dangerous." Louise looked at them sternly.

"We're not *pursuing* anything," Ida lied. "We just wanted to see what was in this secret section of the greenhouse."

"Uh-huh." Louise glared at them, indicating she didn't believe a word Ida said.

"I guess you'll have to verify that he was seen misting his plants by all the various witnesses," Elspeth said.

"What a great idea. I never would have thought of that." Louise's voice dripped with sarcasm.

"Right, then we'll be on our way." Elspeth turned to Ida. "I think this calls for a spot of tea, don't you?"

CHAPTER 13

*I*da was filled with disappointment as they walked back to the flower show. There were still a few hours left, and they wanted to see the nighttime display, in which the entire show would be lit up with those twinkly white lights. Ida wasn't quite as excited about that now, her frustration over not being able to capture the killer overshadowing everything.

"Now what?" Elspeth asked. "We're running out of suspects."

"Kenneth could still be the killer. The police must have had something on him. Otherwise why would they show up?" Ida showed the stamp on the back of her hand to the person at the gate, and they entered.

"Too bad we can't question him further. I suppose we'll have to wait and see if they arrest him."

"I wish we were privy to the same clues as the police." Back home, Ida could always count on finding out what the local police had for clues by asking Mona's granddaughter, Lexy. Lexy was married to one of the police detectives and had ways of finagling clues out of her husband.

"We can glean some of that from their actions." Elspeth turned down the path to the tea tent. "We know that Edith's story must have checked out, or they would have arrested her and not gone to Kenneth's."

"And I suppose they've checked out the family members sufficiently. They are always the first suspects, especially the spouse." The ladies came to an intersecting path and saw Adelaide Timmons pushing a wheelbarrow full of sticks and branches down an adjacent path.

"Maybe we should ask Adelaide if she really did see Kenneth. Hmm, now wait a minute. I think he might have been wrong about that. Adelaide wasn't here before John's murder."

Ida raised a brow. "Maybe Kenneth lied."

"Adelaide! Adelaide!" Elspeth yelled, but the woman must have been too far to hear her. People were looking at them strangely, and Elspeth turned to Ida. "Should we follow her?"

They were almost at the tea tent, and Ida could smell the baked goods. They could always catch up with Adelaide later on. "It will be better to have some tea and form our strategy."

"I agree." Elspeth waved to Violet Crosby as they made their way across the tea tent to one of the available tables near the side. Ida preferred these tables because the tent was open on the sides with more airflow and fewer prying eyes. She didn't think there was anything wrong with putting a few scones into her purse—after all, she'd paid for them—but the fewer people who saw her do it, the fewer judgmental looks she'd have to put up with. Being near the side of the tent allowed her to see what was going on outside the tent, which could always be quite interesting.

"That detective, Louise, is no slouch. She comes off as dippy with that ridiculously old-fashioned trench coat, but she's got some smarts," Ida said once they were seated. "We'd do well to follow her, but I still think we can figure out the killer before they can."

"I think she puts on an act to throw off suspects. Not a bad plan, actually," Elspeth said, glancing outside the tent.

Ida followed her gaze to see a black cat playing

with a monarch butterfly. The cat leapt up repeatedly, pawing at the winged creature, but each time the butterfly flitted out of reach. Ida wondered if the butterfly had escaped from the butterfly tent.

"The police may not have ruled out the family," Ida posited. "Maybe they were just checking out the lead on Kenneth like we were."

"Could be. But Judith and Angie claimed they weren't here. I imagine they had alibis, and I'd think the police would have verified them by now, and if they'd lied, they'd hardly be after Kenneth."

"True." The cat leapt higher, twisting in the air and landing with a soft thud on the brick walkway. The butterfly floated out of reach, taunting the cat much like the killer was lurking around, floating just out of their reach, taunting them. Was it someone they'd talked to already? "If they have ruled out the family, that leaves someone with other motives."

"Like Derek or the rest of the Village Protection Committee," Elspeth said.

Ida glanced at Violet Crosby, who was sitting at a table, sipping tea from a floral bone-china teacup. "Is it any coincidence that a few of the people Kenneth named as being able to verify that he was in the competition tent at the time of Sir John's death are members of the Village Protection Committee?"

Elspeth's brows shot up. "Do you think there could be a conspiracy? That conversation of Edith's that we overheard this morning was quite conspiratorial."

Ida shrugged. "Don't know, but what I do know is I want to try out some of that Battenberg cake. We don't have those back home. Maybe if it's good I can suggest a new pastry for Lexy to try in her bakery." She waved one of the volunteers over, and they ordered.

"We can talk to Violet Crosby and Adelaide pretty easily to verify Kenneth's alibi since they're still right here at the show," Elspeth said. The server brought their order of earl grey tea and a small plate of pastries including scones, Battenberg cake with a lovely fondant type of icing, and some delightful cucumber finger sandwiches. "I doubt Edith will talk to us again, though."

"If they all are in cahoots, then the others might lie," Ida said.

Elspeth considered her words as she munched on a scone. "Maybe we're going about this the wrong way."

"How so?" Ida eyed the plate. Should she have a scone or sandwich? She chose the sandwich because there was no way the two of them could eat everything on the plate, and the scone would keep much better wrapped in a napkin in her purse than the sandwich.

"One of the things we've been trying to figure out is who was inside the flower show early that morning who shouldn't have been here. The killer must have snuck in to murder Sir John. Edith was seen sneaking about in the woods. Kenneth was too. But I heard the police say that they'd interviewed everyone involved, and no one had seen a person who wasn't supposed to be here." Elspeth took a sip of tea. "So maybe we should be looking for someone who was supposed to be here but wasn't where they were supposed to be."

"Ha!" Ida snapped her fingers. "Maybe we shouldn't focus on who saw Kenneth in the tent but who should have been in the tent and didn't see him."

"But who? Derek is the only one I can think of. He was supposed to be at the show early, according to Violet, but he's not one of the people Kenneth named when he was trying to establish an alibi."

"Derek was supposed to be working on Violet Crosby's petunias, I think. We should confirm that, though. Because if those rumors about him meeting with Celia in secret are true, then he might have a strong motive to want Sir John out of the way. He might even have been trying to set Edith up when he mentioned seeing her in the woods!" Ida was quite proud of her deduction, but Elspeth wasn't paying attention. She was busy watching that darn cat play with the butterfly.

"Or, it could be someone else entirely." Elspeth was still watching the cat. "Do you see the paw prints?"

Ida looked over to see wet paw prints leading out of a shallow puddle the cat had stepped in. She supposed the puddle was from the plant next to it being watered. But what was the significance of that? She'd been starting to think that Elspeth was a worthy detecting partner, but now she wasn't so sure. Whoever heard of depending on a cat for clues? Mona, Ruth, and Helen would never have done such a thing.

"Don't tell me you think the cat is giving you a clue. That one that led us out to Kenneth's was just coincidence and—"

Elspeth shot up from the table. "I know who did it! And if my guess is correct, we must hurry before the evidence is destroyed!"

Ida grabbed a napkin and the rest of the scones, which she quickly wrapped and shoved into her purse as she hurried out of the tent after Elspeth.

CHAPTER 14

*E*lspeth kept her ear cocked for the whirring of the wood chipper as she power-walked to the back of the area where the flower show was set up. She'd seen an area there hidden behind a bunch of lattice that had barrels for refuse and machinery. If Adelaide was going to put a wood chipper anywhere, it would be there.

"But how did the cat make you suspect Adelaide?" Ida asked, snapping her large purse shut and power-walking along beside her.

"Not the cat, the footprints. You see, when I got to the show this morning, I cut across that grassy round-about area—you know, the one at the end of the street?"

"With the flowers in it?"

"Yes. At first I wasn't going to cut through—the grass was dewy, and I didn't want my shoes to get wet —but I'd nearly been run over by a car on the round-about and didn't relish walking around it."

"I know! I keep forgetting they come from the wrong direction here!" Ida said.

"Yes, well, when I got to the middle, I stopped to look at those beautiful, tall daisies. I was wondering if some might look good in my garden, and the gates for the show were just opening, so I had a few seconds to tarry."

"And…"

"And that's when I saw the wheelbarrow tracks in the dew. They were coming from the entry gate."

"Okay. So what? We already know that Adelaide picked them for the vases at the gate," Ida said. "They look pretty nice there, too, I might add."

"Don't they?" Elspeth took a sharp right. "But, judging by the state of the tracks, they'd been there about an hour or so, and they were only coming from the front gate, not from the street, and Adelaide lives on the street our cottages are on!"

Ida was silent for a few seconds, then Elspeth heard a sharp intake of breath. "Which means that Adelaide must have lied about getting to the show late!"

"That's right. Edith saw her and assumed that she

was just getting there, but in fact she'd already been there." Elspeth pressed her lips together. "I wonder what she was doing, though. Why was she leaving? Had she forgotten to pick the flowers, or was she trying to remove the murder weapon, and Edith caught her, forcing her to pretend as if she were picking the flowers?"

"But why the wood chipper?"

"When I saw her, she was collecting branches and sticks. Seemed very intent on making sure it was in a pile so that it could be put through the wood chipper after the show closed," Elspeth said. "My guess is that since she couldn't hide the handle of the murder weapon at her house because Edith caught her trying to leave this morning, she plans to chip it up."

"It's brilliant!" Ida said. "Chipping it up in the wood chipper would ensure it was never found."

They rounded a corner and almost barreled into one of the show volunteers with his light-blue-and-yellow vest.

"Hey, ladies! The show is closing. The exit is that way." He pointed in the direction from which they'd just come.

"Sorry, we're on police business," Ida said as she pushed past him.

"Police business?" Elspeth whispered once they'd sped past.

"Well, it's almost police business."

"Speaking of which… maybe we should call them."

"What, and miss out on all the fun and credit? No way!" The sound of a wood chipper split the air, and Ida added, "No time for that now anyway!"

They raced toward the sound. Elspeth was in good condition for a senior citizen, but she had to admit she didn't get much of a chance to run, and she was quite winded when they finally careened around the lattice to find Adelaide Timmons standing next to her wheelbarrow full of branches.

"The exit is the other way," Adelaide shouted as she turned the chipper off and moved in front of the wheelbarrow. She was smiling, and her voice was kind, presumably because she thought they'd just gotten lost.

"We're not looking for the exit," Ida said with authority. She didn't seem the least bit out of breath and, at Elspeth's questioning glance, she added, "I keep myself in tip-top shape with yoga."

"That's nice," Adelaide said. "But the show is over for the day. You can come back tomorrow for the yoga-in-the-gardens event."

Ida's eyes lit up, and for a second Elspeth

wondered if maybe she'd forgotten why they were there.

"Actually, we're not leaving yet." Elspeth craned her neck to see into the wheelbarrow, which was behind Adelaide. It looked like it was filled with branches and other debris. She couldn't see an old handle. As she was looking, a white cat with brilliant-blue eyes trotted over to the wheelbarrow and hopped on top.

"Really, I must insist that you ladies leave. This area isn't part of the show, and it could be dangerous here." Adelaide tried to shove them out of the area, but Elspeth and Ida held their ground.

"I'll say it could be dangerous," Ida said. "There could be a killer here!"

Adelaide froze in her tracks. "Whatever are you talking about?"

"Oh, well, just that a man was killed, and someone did it." Ida moved closer to Adelaide, trying to peek around her at the wheelbarrow. "Did you see the killer, perhaps, when you were here early setting up?"

"I came in late this morning," Adelaide said.

"Oh, that's funny. I thought Kenneth Fairlane said you were in the orchid tent before the start of the show." Ida moved left, and Adelaide moved right to block her.

"I think you ask a lot of questions. You need to

leave." Adelaide stepped toward them, her arm outstretched toward the edge of the lattice as if trying to guide them out.

"Meow!"

The white cat jumped out of the wheelbarrow, tipping it over. Branches and debris tumbled out onto the ground. And one other thing: the broken handle of a garden implement.

"Aha! I knew it!" Elspeth lunged for the handle, but Adelaide was too quick. She shoved Elspeth out of the way, grabbed the handle from the ground, sprinted to the wood chipper, and turned it on.

Ida was fast. She pushed Adelaide away from the machine and pulled on the handle. Elspeth joined her, and the two of them tried to pull the handle away, but Adelaide had a grasp on the D-grip end, and Ida and Elspeth could only grab the splintered shaft.

The deafening sound of the wood chipper knifed the air as they tugged and pulled.

"Let go!" Adelaide yelled. "It's just a spade handle."

"We will not!" Ida yelled back. "This is evidence!"

They were losing the battle. Elspeth realized she'd have to try something else. She let go of the handle, startling Adelaide enough to confuse her, and then she karate-chopped Adelaide's right hand and stomped on her right foot, causing the other woman to drop the handle. Ida scooped it up without a moment's hesitation.

Ida turned admiring eyes to Elspeth. "Good work." Or at least that was what Elspeth thought she'd said. It was hard to tell over the roar of the machine.

"You too," Elspeth returned the compliment.

"Ahhh!" Adelaide let out a cry then lunged for them, and all three of them tumbled to the ground, Ida holding the handle for dear life as Adelaide tried to pry it from her. Elspeth jumped on top to stop her.

"Hold it right there! Nobody move!"

Elspeth recognized the voice right away. The police had come.

Louise shut off the wood chipper and looked down at them, her hands on her hips.

"We caught the killer, and she has the murder weapon!" Ida pointed to Adelaide, who Max was already hauling to her feet.

"Why don't you tell me all about it?" Louise bent to examine the handle while Ida and Elspeth told them how they deduced that Adelaide was the killer and how they'd saved the evidence from the wood chipper.

Louise turned to Adelaide. "Can you explain why you have this?"

"It's just an old piece of a spade."

"Then why put it in the wood chipper?" Max asked.

"I was recycling," Adelaide said.

Louise stood. "Okay, then can you explain why you lied to us about coming in late this morning? Several people saw you here."

"I... well... they must be wrong."

"They're not wrong," Max said. "We know you had means, motive, and opportunity."

"I... he was... the sale was going to close down the show! I don't have anything else since my husband died!" Adelaide burst into tears.

Elspeth felt a teeny bit sorry for her, but honestly, the woman could have gotten another hobby. Or maybe even a cat.

"No one in the village wanted the sale," Adelaide blubbered. "I was doing the whole village a favor."

"I'm sure you saw it that way, but maybe Sir John didn't," Louise said. "Tell us how it happened."

"I begged Sir John not to sell. But he was determined. Wanted to travel the world with Celia." Adelaide's mouth twisted. "He had plenty of money. He could have just given the house to Angie. Even Celia agreed. But no. He didn't want to leave it to her because he didn't agree with her artsy lifestyle."

"So you lured him here to kill him," Ida prompted.

"No! I invited him in to see the show early before anyone else. I was hoping that once he remembered how beautifully it was set up and how those showing their plants depended on the show and loved it, he'd have a change of heart. But he didn't." Adelaide's expression turned hard, and she wiped tears from her cheeks.

"So you whacked him over the head," Ida said.

"We argued, and things got heated. Before I knew it, he was lying facedown in the koi pond, and I was holding half a spade in my hand." Adelaide glanced at the handle. "I can't believe it broke. He had a really hard head."

"But why keep the handle?" Max asked as he put cuffs on her. Adelaide didn't seem to even notice. She was engrossed in telling her story. Elspeth figured she must have been resigned to her fate.

"It splintered, and I bled. I couldn't leave it. I was going to take it home to bury in the yard, but when I saw Edith coming out on the path from the woods, I knew she would think it was suspicious for me to be going home at that time. That's when I came up with the wood chipper plan."

"But by then, the show was opening, and you couldn't run the wood chipper because it would be too disruptive to the show," Elspeth said.

"That's right. So I just hid the handle with the debris we'd collected from fallen branches and such. I figured I'd just chop it up tonight, and that would be the end of it."

"That would have been a good plan," Max said. "If not for two curious senior citizens."

The tone of the sergeant's voice almost sounded like he was proud of them, and Ida and Elspeth beamed at him.

"Two curious senior citizens who told the volunteer in the path they were with the police." Louise didn't sound so proud of them, and their beams faded.

"Well, that is how we got here so fast," Max said.

Louise shrugged. "I suppose they deserve some credit. We were coming to question Adelaide about some of the discrepancies in her statement, but if the volunteer didn't point us in the direction that the 'other police' had gone, we wouldn't have run and might not have gotten here before the handle was turned into chips."

Elspeth and Ida beamed again.

Louise scowled at them. "Instead of congratulating you on a job well done, I should be arresting you two for impersonating police officers!"

"Jeez, can't a girl get a break here?" Ida put on the charm. "We did help a little, didn't we?"

Louise snorted. "I won't throw you in jail, mostly

because I'm afraid you might miss your flight out of here. Just promise you won't do it again."

"We won't," Ida and Elspeth said at the same time. Elspeth wasn't sure about Ida, but she was crossing her fingers behind her back.

"Fine, then. When do you ladies leave town?"

Elspeth had had such a fun time that she hated the idea of leaving, but she was anxious to get home to her cats. "Next Tuesday."

"Me too," Ida said. "We should compare flight times. Maybe we can share a ride to the airport."

"Sounds good," Elspeth said.

"Yeah, sounds good to me too." Louise herded them toward the exit. "Have a lovely trip home. Hopefully I won't be seeing you before you leave."

"THOSE TWO LADIES SURE ARE CHARACTERS." Max smiled as he watched Ida and Elspeth leave.

"They were kind of fun." Louise hated to admit it, but she had found the two old ladies charming in an irritating sort of way.

"I don't think they're very fun at all," Adelaide muttered. She'd been calmly accepting of her fate and had given them no trouble once the confession was out.

"I'm glad they didn't come to any harm. We'll just let them think they had the case all wrapped up," Louise said.

"They probably think they led us to the killer and we'd never have solved the case without them," Max said.

Louise frowned. "Well, they didn't. We had a hunch it was Adelaide from the start." Louise pressed her lips together and glanced at their retreating backs. "Though I will admit that they did help us out in getting information."

"And they stopped the killer from destroying the evidence." Max pointed to the spade handle.

"Yes, they came in handy," Louise admitted. "I hope they go home and tell all their friends how they solved the case, but I don't want to see them back here any time soon."

"Keeping them out of trouble was a lot of work." Max took Adelaide by the elbow and propelled her down the path to their police car waiting at the entry gate.

"You can say that again. I feel sorry for the police in the towns they live in back in the States." Louise followed with the spade, which she'd put in a large paper evidence bag that she'd produced from one of the deep pockets of her trench coat.

Max laughed. "They must have their hands full. They did get the villagers to talk, though. You sure you don't want to hire on some little old lady consultants just for that purpose?"

"Don't go getting any ideas. Two miniature Miss Marples in one lifetime are enough!"

ive days later, Elspeth and Ida sat on Elspeth's patio, a steaming pot of tea and a plate of tiny salmon luncheon sandwiches on the table in front of them. It was the day before they were supposed to fly back home, and they were taking a break from packing.

"I think we had a pretty good week. I quite liked it," Elspeth said.

"The flower show was lovely, and we caught a killer—what's not to like about that?" Ida nibbled one of the tiny sandwiches. The only complaint she had was that the food was in such tiny portions. She'd be happy to get home to regular-sized meals and snacks. "We must get together when we get back to New Hampshire. I want you to meet the other members of the Ladies' Detective Club. I'm nominating you for an honorary membership."

Elspeth blushed with pleasure. "And I'd love to show you around Mystic Notch. You could meet all my cats, and I'm sure you'd find things in the Notch quite magical."

A gaggle of cats had been watching them on the patio, and one in particular—a gray-and-black cat with fluffy fur that Elspeth had said was a Norwegian Forest cat—had been lurking around Ida's ankles.

Ida hadn't cared much for cats before, but she had to admit that it had seemed like the cats were sending subtle messages when they'd been investigating the murder. She looked down at the Forest cat, wondering if she should consider adopting one when she got home.

"He won't bite you, you know." Elspeth made clucking noises, and an orange-striped cat came to her, taking a tiny smidgen of salmon from her fingers and jumping into her lap. "They're quite wonderful and loving creatures."

Ida wasn't so sure about that. But the look of contentment on Elspeth's face as she petted the cat made her wonder just what the other woman saw in the furry creatures. She pinched a smidgen of salmon out of her sandwich and imitated the noises Elspeth had made. The fluffy, gray cat jumped in her lap, surprising her so much that she almost fell over backwards.

The cat was surprisingly light. Its silky fur and the purring sound it made were rather enjoyable. Maybe Elspeth was right. Ida could get used to this.

"See? I knew you would like them. Very intelligent creatures and fun to hold." Elspeth picked hers up and cuddled it. "Almost like a baby but better because you don't have to change diapers."

Ida petted the cat in her lap thoughtfully. She liked babies but hated diapers. "Speaking of babies, it seems like everything is going to end well for the Hastings family. I mean, except for Sir John being killed and all."

"Indeed! I'd been wondering what that mysterious statement Celia had made—'a big change for the family'—was all about, but I had no idea that it was about a baby!" Elspeth took a bite of the sandwich.

"Poor thing. I feel bad for suspecting her now. The thought never occurred to me that she was seeing Derek for his spiritual healing talents, to help her conceive. Sad that Sir John won't see the baby be born."

"It is sad, but that baby will have a loving family, especially with Judith and Angie moving in to help."

Elspeth shooed the cat out of her lap and bent down to pet one of the others.

In addition to the news of the baby and why Celia had been seeing Derek in secret, they'd also discovered through the village gossip that Celia had secretly been buying Angie's paintings through a third party. Apparently she wasn't the typical evil stepmother. She'd been trying to persuade Sir John to reconcile with Angie and to give Angie and Judith free rein of the house while they went on their travels. It was John who wanted to sell, and now that he was gone, Celia had immediately squashed the sale, much to the delight of the members of the Village Protection Committee.

"I think it's sweet that they will all live in the house and raise the baby as a family. Even Angie seemed delighted. And that place is big enough for three families." Ida bent down to pet another cat. This one was pure gray with greenish-gold eyes that stared at her as if it knew what she was thinking. The one in her lap let out a protesting meow. Apparently it didn't like Ida giving attention to the other cat.

"If only Adelaide hadn't resorted to murder, Celia might have gotten John to change his mind before the sale went through. What a waste." Elspeth looked at the empty plate. "I sure wish we had some of those scones for dessert."

Ida shoved the cat out of her lap and reached for her purse on the ground beside her chair. "I can fix us up. I got these this morning at the tea shop in town." She plopped the purse onto the table, pulled a napkin out, and opened it carefully, revealing two golden-brown scones.

Elspeth's left brow shot up, but she tentatively took a scone and put it on her plate. "I suppose it *is* still fresh."

Ida nodded. "It is. They taste just as good from the purse as they do from a bakery box."

Elspeth bit into it. "Oh, this is very good! What a novel idea."

"Thank you."

Elspeth gobbled down another bite then eyed the oversized, tan patent-leather purse that was still sitting on the table. "Where did you get your purse? I might need a bigger purse when I get home. The tea shop in town has the most delicious scones, and I always want to take some leftovers home but feel funny asking for a box for half a scone."

"Macy's." Ida smiled, happy to pass along that little trick to her new friend.

They finished their scones and brushed the crumbs

off. Ida was sad to have to get back to packing. "Well, looks like the village will stay as quaint as it is. The flower show will still go on. I hear Judith will be in charge now."

"We should make a plan to come back next year. Violet Crosby told me that Celia gave Kenneth permission to hunt the estate for orchids, and he's entering the ones he found in the contest next year."

"That sounds like a great idea." Ida raised her teacup and held it out to Elspeth. "To new friends and new traditions."

They clinked rims, and Elspeth added, "And to new crimes to solve."

****

I HOPE you enjoyed meeting Ida and Elspeth in this story. Ida is from the Lexy Baker Series of humorous culinary cozy mysteries, and Elspeth is from the Mystic Notch series that has mystery solving cats. You can find out more about those series here:

Lexy Baker Cozy Mystery Series

Mystic Notch Paranormal Cozy Mysteries

. . .

FIND out about my latest books and how to get discounts on them by signing up at:

https://leighanndobbscozymysteries.gr8.com

IF YOU WANT to receive a text message alert on your cell phone for new releases , text COZYMYSTERY to 88202 (sorry, this only works for US cell phones!)

JOIN my VIP readers group on Facebook

https://www.facebook.com/groups/ldobbsreaders

ALSO BY LEIGHANN DOBBS

Cozy Mysteries

Mystic Notch

Cat Cozy Mystery Series

* * *

Ghostly Paws

A Spirited Tail

A Mew To A Kill

Paws and Effect

Probable Paws

Whisker of a Doubt

Wrong Side of the Claw

Oyster Cove Guesthouse

Cat Cozy Mystery Series

***

A Twist in the Tail

A Whisker in the Dark

Kate Diamond Mystery Adventures

***

Hidden Agemda (Book 1)

Ancient Hiss Story (Book 2)

Heist Society (Book 3)

Silver Hollow

Paranormal Cozy Mystery Series

***

A Spell of Trouble (Book 1)

Spell Disaster (Book 2)

Nothing to Croak About (Book 3)

Cry Wolf (Book 4)

Shear Magic (Book 5)

Mooseamuck Island

Cozy Mystery Series

* * *

A Zen For Murder

A Crabby Killer

A Treacherous Treasure

Blackmoore Sisters

Cozy Mystery Series

* * *

Dead Wrong

Dead & Buried

Dead Tide

Buried Secrets

Deadly Intentions

A Grave Mistake

Spell Found

Fatal Fortune

Hidden Secrets

Lexy Baker

Cozy Mystery Series

* * *

Murder at the Ice Ball (Book 3)

A Murderous Affair (Book 4)

Hazel Martin Historical Mystery Series

***

Murder at Lowry House (book 1)

Murder by Misunderstanding (book 2)

Sam Mason Mysteries

(As L. A. Dobbs)

***

Telling Lies (Book 1)

Keeping Secrets (Book 2)

Exposing Truths (Book 3)

Betraying Trust (Book 4)

Killing Dreams (Book 5)

Rockford Security Series

***

Deadly Betrayal (Book 1)

Fatal Games (Book 2)

Treacherous Seduction (Book 3)

Calculating Desires (Book 4)

Wicked Deception (Book 5)

Criminal Intentions (Book 6)

Romantic Comedy

***

Corporate Chaos Series

In Over Her Head (book 1)

Can't Stand the Heat (book 2)

What Goes Around Comes Around (book 3)

Careful What You Wish For (4)

Contemporary Romance

***

Reluctant Romance

Sweet Romance (Written As Annie Dobbs)

Firefly Inn Series

***

Another Chance (Book 1)

Another Wish (Book 2)

Hometown Hearts Series

***

No Getting Over You (Book 1)

A Change of Heart (Book 2)

Sweet Mountain Billionaires

***

Jaded Billionaire (Book 1)

A Billion Reasons Not To Fall In Love (Book 2)

***

Sweetrock Sweet and Spicy Cowboy Romance

Some Like It Hot

Too Close For Comfort

Regency Romance

***

Scandals and Spies Series:

Kissing The Enemy

Deceiving the Duke

Tempting the Rival

Charming the Spy

Pursuing the Traitor

Captivating the Captain

The Unexpected Series:

An Unexpected Proposal

An Unexpected Passion

Dobbs Fancytales:

Dobbs Fancytales Boxed Set Collection

————

Western Historical Romance

***

Goldwater Creek Mail Order Brides:

Faith

American Mail Order Brides Series:

Chevonne: Bride of Oklahoma

—————————————————

Magical Romance with a Touch of Mystery

***

Something Magical

Curiously Enchanted

ABOUT THE AUTHOR

USA Today best-selling Author, Leighann Dobbs, has had a passion for reading since she was old enough to hold a book, but she didn't put pen to paper until much later in life. After a twenty-year career as a software engineer, with a few side trips into selling antiques and making jewelry, she realized you can't make a living reading books, so she tried her hand at writing them and discovered she had a passion for that, too! She lives in New Hampshire with her husband, Bruce, their trusty Chihuahua mix, Mojo, and beautiful rescue cat, Kitty.

Find out about her latest books and how to get discounts on them by signing up at:

https://leighanndobbscozymysteries.gr8.com

If you want to receive a text message alert on your cell phone for new releases , text COZYMYSTERY to 88202 (sorry, this only works for US cell phones!)

Join the VIP readers group on Facebook
https://www.facebook.com/groups/ldobbsreaders

This is a work of fiction.

None of it is real. All names, places, and events are products of the author's imagination. Any resemblance to real names, places, or events are purely coincidental, and should not be construed as being real.